"*Carissima*," he intoned, breathless. "Finally, we can be together. All week I have waited for this moment, wanting you, knowing that you wanted me. Yet, I fclt I could do nothing until the very night of my triumph."

His slightly damp hands glided over my skin, squeezing; his lips touched my shoulders, my arms, finally the tops of my breasts. His tongue was a faint whisper on my flesh. Then his mouth was on mine, his tongue probing, intertwining; startled, elated, I allowed him everything without resistance.

Now his hands had purpose reaching for the thin rhinestone straps of my dress, lowering them over my shoulders. My dress slipped to the floor with a rustle that was drowned in my ears by the throbbing beat of my own heart and the rush of my blood.

"I knew it would be this way," he whispered, "that when your dress came off there would be nothing more covering your beautiful white skin …"

Love's Illusion

ANONYMOUS

cover design: stella by design contact: stellabydesign@aol.com

Chapter 1

I should have been elated when they told me about the interview with Alfredo Carobino. Not just an interview, but a full week of dogging his tracks, living his daily routine along with him, capturing his every nuance on camera. A week with one of the world's greatest living tenors. Of course, it didn't hurt that he's also a world-class hunk of masculine flesh with appetites that had become legendary even in jaded entertainment circles.

Just Carobino and me. And the opera's publicist. And a television crew. No wonder I was less than thrilled. What chance would I have to be alone with this romantic icon? And realistically, what would I do if the opportunity arose—turn into one of those hysterical opera groupies who throw themselves at his feet and the more select parts of his anatomy?

Not hardly.

After all, I'm a professional, and a media personality, in my own right. My stature, and my dignity, have always been important to me.

I am Elizabeth Renard, star of local news, weather, sports, and film at eleven.

Actually, I'm not an anchorperson, just one of the reporters. But once you're on television regularly, even on a local station, people recognize you and you get star treatment. I've become accustomed to it. If you press me, I'll even admit to liking it, although I pretend not to.

Of course there are drawbacks. You don't dare leave the house without makeup, even to go to the corner store, or you're likely to overhear those dreaded words: "She's much prettier on television."

So it's a trap, that little bit of fame and recognition. You're never quite free. People own a part of you. It's nearly impossible to do the simplest things unobserved. But that's the challenge, isn't it? I accept it, and I've gloried in my bit of fame. I use it; I bask in it. And all the while I know, innately, that such power exacts a price, that it's only an illusion. I brood about it sometimes, analyze it always. I try to put my finger on who I am. Why I am. I'm not sure I've been entirely successful.

I know this—I'm extremely pretty. I don't say it out of vanity. It's simply the truth. Some people think I'm beautiful. The miracle of makeup probably has something to do with it—the ability to create illusions. Of course, that's one advantage of being on television. You have to look your best, because someone in a plush office upstairs feels it impacts on the ratings. So professionals teach you how to strengthen the illusion. And they even do it for you on those occasions when the new director bestows upon you the high honor of being a substitute anchor.

I try to be honest. My looks have made me a television reporter, have helped me to be assigned more screen time than many of my...shall we say, less radiant, associates? I've few regrets, although looking the way I do probably kept me from being a concert pianist. But I suppose I should be philosophical about it. A second- maybe even third-rate television reporter makes a lot more money than most first-rate pianists...and certainly wields a lot more power.

And I have no way of knowing if I would ever have been first-rate at the keyboard.

I am only what I am.

I was the sort of child smiling teachers invariably cast as the princess in school plays. Sometimes I think it had as much to do with my hair as my face. It's raven black and long, with just enough natural curl in it. My mother loved to brush it, to make it shine until she could see stars in it, she would say. I'm not quite as devoted to its care as she was. But it still cascades to the middle of my back and has a nice sheen to it most of the time, although I suspect the stars in it have long since winked out.

Being everyone's princess is not the delight it should be. It's a world of responsibility when you're a little girl. People seem to expect so much when they've proclaimed you royalty.

And then when you grow up and you're not a princess after all, your subjects gradually disappear.

It takes a lot of adjustment. It also makes you painfully aware, like a slap in the face, that power—*power*—creates royalty. And in the awful light of that revelation, you can never be the same.

I suppose my private life isn't quite as glamorous as my public one. Mother never meant for me to be alone the way I am. She wanted me to be her little princess, until my prince arrived. She didn't cling. She intended to hand me over to that prince, the way she'd been delivered to my father by her own parents.

I never knew my father. But I believed my mother when she told me they'd been blissfully happy. Until he got the call to fight in a war from which he never returned. Mother never stopped mourning him. And she hoped that some day I would love a man so much that he would become the lasting adoration of my life, just as my father had been to her.

Oh, Mother meant well. But for her, loving and a continual state of bereavement were a kind of happiness. She wore professional widowhood like a comforting shawl. That, too, had its effect on me.

She meant to teach me to love, to open myself to the kind of emotion that only a man and a woman can share. But instead, she frightened me with her reminiscences of bliss and fairy-tale romance. What good was love in absentia? I loved a father I could never know. I became afraid that loving a man meant that he would leave you or be taken from you.

I'm in my mid-thirties now. That's as much as I can say, without the station publicist tearing her hair out. I've enjoyed a few moderately satisfying relationships with men, plus a couple of death-defying one-night stands. And since I meet a lot of men in my line of work, I have as many dates as I have time for. But I don't have a lot of time, or much tolerance for men with wilted self-images. A romantic dinner at L'Etoile, interrupted by my beeper and a subsequent rush to a three-alarm fire, can be hell on a man's ego and libido...especially if "film at eleven" wasn't exactly what we'd been planning for the evening's climax.

But, hey, that's the news biz. I approach it the way I approach love. Make it matter while it lasts. You never know when it will go away. And there are perks, like spending a whole week with Alfredo Carobino. Not as one of the call girls that are always arranged for him by the posh hotels he frequents. Not as a sexual thing for his dispassionate use, to be

8

paid off and forgotten when the last aria has been sung. But as a professional reporter, worthy of his respect as a person.

Carobino would remember me, I vowed.

"You're picking up Carobino at his hotel Monday, promptly at noon," Stan, my assignment editor, told me. "Plan on lots of pictures," he smiled crookedly. "*Il signore* doesn't want to strain his vocal chords answering a lot of mundane questions. Maybe you can find out who he's been sleeping with."

Good old Stan. You could always count on him to concentrate on the important things.

"Anyway, try not to swoon on camera or salivate on the microphone. I know how you get about these guys."

He was still smiling as I gave him the finger and left his office swaying my hips seductively.

I didn't swoon when I met Carobino. A healthy dose of reality saw to that. He wasn't nearly as splendid up close as he appears on stage. Being in the illusion business, I shouldn't have been as surprised as I was. Carobino was getting jowly as he approached his fortieth year. The critics had begun pointing out that some of his high notes left a bit to be desired in texture and pitch. But overall, his voice had remained strong. And he could truly act—a rarity on the opera stage. More importantly, in a pair of tights, he could match form with the best of the male ballet dancers.

God, I loved his buns. I'd fantasized about running my hands over their smooth firmness. I'd dreamed of rubbing my breasts across them, feeling my nipples grow hard at the contact of my skin on his. Then I'd turn him over and wrap my lips around the huge shaft that I knew would be there. I'd pump him mercilessly with my hand and tease the silky head of his cock with my tongue until I felt him expand to the point of explosion. Then he'd sing just for me as he coated my throat with the torrent of his passion. I'd hoped he'd be wearing tight-fitting pants.

Baggy trousers. Loose Armani jacket.

Unfair, I cried in my soul as I introduced myself.

"So you are the lovely lady who spends the week with me. What could be happier?" he crooned, actually kissing my hand. I was careful not to roll my eyes. He'd have to do better than that. No clichés or second-rate Valentinos would be accepted here. Mere manner would touch neither my heart nor my libido.

His face hadn't lost its chiselled handsomeness, although added pounds had begun to smooth the edges. In a few years he might become just another fat tenor, I thought with some regret. But even with slight shadows under his eyes, at what for him was an early hour, his appeal remained largely undiminished.

And his smile. Oh, lord, his smile. Let him just smile at me like that again, I quivered, and I might become hopeless. Yes, the lady did protest too much. I was hunting for faults, for the crack in the façade. And still I was smitten, just like any other silly woman might have been.

For his favor I would gladly die with him or for him.

"We'll need to get a shot of you leaving the hotel," I said, my calmness belying my inner turmoil. I was really good at my job.

"Whatever is best," he said. "I am completely in your hands." Oh, he was good. My heart fluttered. My hands trembled. I felt warmth rising in my face, up my thighs. I was Mimi on a cold Paris night, waiting to be warmed, caressed by Rodolfo.

This is absurd, I chided myself. For God's sake, I'd interviewed Warren Beatty. And he hadn't even made my eyelashes flutter, much less my heart. No sane woman goes gaga over a tenor, I insisted. A baritone, maybe. But a tenor?

I've always been such a sucker for the wrong men. They didn't die on me. They didn't fade away. They just turned into aging messes that never quite lived up to my expectations.

Well, I was glad I'd seen Carobino in the bright light of day. Sure he was good to look at, even better to listen to. And as we followed him to his fittings, watched his people glue wigs to his receding hairline, I admitted that for a media person who was herself the product of packaging, I had certainly fallen for the lot of it. And what of it? What if the best wig masters in the country were making him the man who could fulfill my dreams? Didn't the costumes of the hero make him grander than life?

Reality can be so much more disappointing, especially when Italian suits do not masculine magnificence make. I decided to discard common sense and let my feelings enjoy the ride.

By the time we were halfway through a piano rehearsal, I knew that Carobino was singing only for me. His voice soared above the seats of the auditorium, seeking the heavens. The lighting accentuated his presence; he virtually generated his own aura. The knowledge that this was simply stage magic created for a willing audiences did little to lessen Carobino's impact upon me. I was more smitten as each day went by. And I was devastated to think that it would soon be over.

I did my job. I was there for all of his rehearsals, all of his fittings. The opera owned his time, his life, but at least I was able to share in it for a little while.

On rehearsal days Carobino changed his habits and rose early. To accommodate him, the production staff began early, then took a long lunch. At four P.M. the rehearsals would begin anew.

Each day, as the break period loomed, I expected he would ask me to accompany him to his nearby hotel room for a private encounter.

But I was disappointed each time.

He was charming, even seductive in an offhand manner, with me as with all women. But when the lunch break arrived each day, he would distractedly beg, "*Permiso*, I must rest." And he would return to his room, with my camera crew in tow before he'd disappear through the doors of his suite. I found out later, from a bit of overheard conversation between stagehands, that it wasn't only lunch that waited for him during those "rest" periods.

By the fourth day, I was sure that the crew was observing with amusement my every reaction to Carobino's seeming disinterest. I tried to maintain my professional demeanor. But I was not only jealous, I was paranoid about the impression I was making and the gossip I was serving up for the entire television station.

Seeing Carobino strut and preen on stage only heightened my need. He would pose so that his girded manhood showed to its best advantage.

The image would present itself to me again and again, especially at night. I would lie awake, naked beneath my sheets, thinking of Carobino in his suite entertaining some slut from the streets.

It was unfair that the best I could summon for my needs was my trusty vibrator. I could almost hear Carobino's voice as I would run its cool, blunt tip along my inner thighs. With my right hand I'd massage myself, first inserting one finger, then two, then three, until I'd lubricated the well between my legs. I'd slide the dildo back and forth, moving it in slow, sensuous circles. I'd imagine my virtuoso lover flicking his tongue over my throbbing clitoris and separating the folds of skin with his darting strokes. Then I'd insert the vibrator in my pussy and try to establish a motion that mimicked the action of a hot, jerking cock. I'd withdraw it, lick it clean, then reinsert it until I finally managed to build to a furious climax. It was never very satisfying, and I'd curse myself for even bothering to get worked up. It only accentuated my need to have Carobino's rock-hard prick in me.

Two days later the opera season opened, with Carobino in his signature role of Alfredo Germont, perhaps the only man who could steal *La Traviata* from even the finest of Violettas. And among this cast, in which the soprano was not top caliber, Carobino shone. The elite of San Francisco would undoubtedly hammer at the opera house doors each night of the engagement to be touched by his radiance.

I was absorbed by his every movement as I watched Violetta die in his arms. The romantic in me, the fantasy person who could live as I never had, felt the passion, the sorrow of her passing, wondering what it would be like to love a man so desperately, to die so nearly happy, with the conviction of his undying love.

Opening night had given me the excuse for my deepest décolletage, not that I had that much cleavage to show. But I do have exquisite shoulders and a perfectly curving back, and a cute little ass, as I've been told by the men I've been with.

Dressing this way wasn't the sort of thing that Mother's little princess would have done. And it's not the sort of thing an objective, professional reporter should have done. I was grateful that I had a weekend crew at the opening. The camera operator was a woman who could understand how I felt and who wasn't the sort to enjoy it as a joke at my expense.

I knew this was my last chance—the last night of the shoot. I had been given clearance to come back-stage, to stand in the wings. The camera had to be kept at a distance, but I was right there with Carobino.

He'd been so focused on the performance to come, so trying to cope with barely concealed stage fright, that he hardly seemed to see me. What a waste, I thought—I'd dressed for a bunch of leering stage-hands. Yet I was even more enchanted by Carobino's case of nerves. The bravado of the star was nowhere to be seen, only a boy's terror as he prepared to recite in front of the class.

Once he was on stage it was all different, of course. He was Carobino. He was Alfredo. He was love, pas-sion, fantasy. And how he sang. By the end of the first act Violetta burned for Alfredo.

And so did I. How I dreamed all through the sec-ond act that it was the two of us in that country cot-tage and that the tragedy of the opera never arrived. No misguided parent would ever have separated the two of us.

During the first intermission, I'd stood in the lobby with the crew, soliciting audience reactions. We were preparing to do more of the same during the second break when Carobino swept through the wings on the way to his dressing room. Almost as an afterthought he grabbed my arm and swept me along with him.

I won't debase what I felt by calling it anything less than sublime. When we reached his dressing room, he closed and locked the door behind us. And then he locked me in his arms.

14

"*Carissima*," he intoned, breathless. "Finally, we can be together. All week I have waited for this moment, wanting you, knowing that you wanted me. Yet, I felt I could do nothing until the very night of my triumph."

His slightly damp hands glided over my skin, squeezing; his lips touched my shoulders, my arms, finally the tops of my breasts. His tongue was a faint whisper on my flesh. Then his mouth was on mine, his tongue probing, intertwining; startled, elated, I allowed him everything without resistance.

Now his hands had purpose reaching for the thin rhinestone straps of my dress, lowering them over my shoulders. My dress slipped to the floor with a rustle that was drowned in my ears by the throbbing beat of my own heart and the rush of my blood.

"I knew it would be this way," he whispered, "that when your dress came off there would be nothing more covering your beautiful white skin." He lowered his head and took one of my nipples in his mouth, gently biting it while cupping my breast with his hand. It responded to his ministrations by growing beneath his tongue. I gasped as waves of pleasure rolled over me. I hadn't expected this…this…dream made real. But I had no intention of ending the dream either.

He guided me toward a green velvet chaise, lowering me onto it with gentle pressure on my shoulders, his eyes hungrily consuming my nakedness. Those eyes that had looked into those of royalty, political leaders, the cream of society, now roved over me, settling for a moment on the wispy darkness between my legs as if sensing the wetness there. I thought he'd penetrate me with his look alone. He shrugged off his costume jacket. He looked delicious in his satin vest, ruffled shirt, and tight, tight pants. He knew this of course, and rather than destroy the illusion by disrobing, he only began to open his buttons of the eighteenth century version of a fly.

I watched. Transfixed.

"No codpiece, you see," he laughed.

I saw nothing. I was in a kind of delirium.

"Not like those ballet dancers. What singers have is real. We are men. And you are such a beautiful woman. We must be together."

He reclined on the chaise, pulling me toward him. My mind, which had shut down from the moment he took my arm in the wings, reawakened for just a second. "I want to," I heard myself saying. "Yes, I've wanted to since we met, since long before we met." My hands had already taken on a life of their own, as they unfastened the vest and the ruffled shirt. But I added with the nobility of the most tragic of opera heroines, "There isn't time. You must be back on stage."

"No, no, my darling. There is nothing to worry about. We have forever until Alfredo must make his entrance on stage. I am never late for my entrance. They will wait for me. I am Carobino. Only our entrance matters now."

He pulled me toward him. His head was already moving down as his hands finally settled on my breasts, kneading them almost painfully. My eyes found the ceiling as his tongue wended its way through my pubic hair, performing the *entr'acte* for the exquisite scene to come. His lips and tongue descended on my cunt, licking, biting as he found the source of my pleasure. His tongue, like a snake, separated my lips and slithered along each side as I began to writhe with abandon.

And then my mind, damn my mind, began working again. I realized that Carobino had played this scene, this interlude, a thousand times. That when it was over and he'd finished the run of the opera, maybe even before, he wouldn't even remember who I was.

Should it matter? I asked myself. This was my moment, my dream.

My nipples hardened as he moved upward and reached for the combs that held my hair back. They dropped to the floor and my hair cascaded, just as I had intended it to. Carobino moaned softly, stroked my hair, my body.

Over the loudspeaker, I could hear the first bars of Violetta's tragic aria. She would never have Alfredo again, except to die in his arms. But she would die happy, because he had loved her. I would never have Alfredo again, but I would live more happily, I told myself, because he had made love to me, if only for one time.

Panting, he pulled me to him, ready to enter me, I knew. I braced myself in expectation of the thrust, spread myself wide to better let him impale me on his huge pole. I waited, then felt the whisper of a passage.

Crazed with lust, I waited for him to fill me.

But there was nothing. I felt nothing.

I looked down. Something minute dangled from the fly of Carobino's pants. Well, perhaps it wasn't quite so minute as it was soft.

Oh, Christ, my soul and my libido cried. Not this, not now.

Undaunted, Carobino took my head and guided my mouth to his inert member. Yes, of course, I thought. After two acts of the performance he'd expended so much energy, what should I expect?

I took his cock in my mouth, cupping it with my lips as I'd fantasized I would. I bathed its length with my hot saliva, sucking in as hard as I could, licking the underside of the shaft. I knew that no man could resist this treatment and still call himself a man. As if in response to my thought, I felt his manhood begin to stir, stiffening and thickening at the same time.

"Hurry, *Carissima*," he said, barely audible. Over the backstage speaker a tinny voice squawked, "Mr. Carobino, five minutes until entrance. Five minutes, please."

I doubled my efforts and was rewarded with more of him. As much as there would be, I realized.

Aroused now, Carobino suddenly shifted position, popping his erect penis from my mouth. Wanting to see, I propped myself up on my elbows. His not-very-impressive prick hovered at the entrance to my wet and waiting pussy. I could feel the head as it parted my lips, but sensation ended there.

"Hurry, my darling," he stage whispered.

Seconds later, his body jerked three times. He sighed with an almost animal-like contentment, then withdrew without further delay or comment. Then he pushed me away, not so much harshly, as indifferently. "And now, my dearest, you must dress quickly and go, and send my man to me. He will be just outside the door. I must change my costume."

Stunned, I did as I was told. And then I raced down the hall to the nearest ladies' lounge to pull myself back together, avoiding the laughing eyes of the stage crew.

I tried to hold back the tears of shame and frustration.

When I emerged from my sanctuary, I fancied that I looked nearly normal. But as I walked down the hall, I felt the eyes of the men. I felt myself redden, just as I had on a day long ago when I'd stood in front of the all-male panel of judges for the Miss Corporate San Francisco competition.

I felt naked then, too.

Chapter 2

When I graduated from Cal, it took me a whole two weeks to discover that such academic achievement was all but irrelevant in the real world. Not that anything in San Francisco can accurately be termed the real world. If ever there was fantasyland, albeit with a slant toward the bizarre, San Francisco was it.

So, fresh out of the University of California, I enthusiastically charged into the world of grown-ups. My degree was in hand, the future lay open before me.

Oh, was I ever ready for a fall.

How many words a minute do you type? That was all they ever asked at the agencies. My skills on the piano didn't translate well to a typewriter keyboard. Some form of rebellion, I suppose.

I tested at about forty words a minute. With lots of mistakes. That meant no jobs.

But I was young and pretty. And my sorority, along with my mother's earlier training, had given me a ladylike air. Plus, I knew how to dress for success, or seduction. I couldn't help it. *Vogue* was our sorority bible.

After nearly two months of searching, of fruitless

interviews, of passes made and ducked, of being told by snotty personnel functionaries that I just didn't have the proper qualifications, of returning each day to my mother's house to face her eternally chipper disposition, I found my niche. Elizabeth Renard, with her near-genius IQ, her near-Phi Beta Kappa grades, her concert-level talent—was going to be the receptionist at Future Vista Enterprises.

Let the choir say Amen.

I was the crème de la crème of the country, as so many of my professors and music instructors, not to mention many of the fraternity boys I'd dated, had assured me. So, I thought, as I settled behind my desk during my first day at FVE, this must be where the cream settles.

It was not the exciting future I had imagined for myself those lastfew months of my emergence from childhood. But then, I hadn't actually imagined much of anything. So I concluded at first that my lack of immediate success was my own fault.

But, no, I was smart enough to realize that the damned system was to blame. There were only two places in the world for women then—in the home or behind a typewriter. There was also nursing, but that's not a profession for someone who faints at the sight of blood. And I certainly didn't intend to wash someone's bedpan.

Teaching would have been logical for me, but there had never been a shortage of music teachers. Also, the idea of teaching tone-deaf little monsters who thought the classics began with the Beatles was not my idea of a career.

My friends suggested modeling. And I might have given that a try, but I wasn't tall enough, and I probably wasn't thin enough. No tits and flat asses were in; I just didn't fancy starvation as a way of life.

So there I was at FVE, answering phones, transferring calls, doing a little light (very light) typing.

Of course, I was also ogled by executives, who undressed me with their eyes and fucked me in their minds. Back then the words "sexual harassment" would have elicited nothing more than a blank stare. My bosses knew what I'd been hired for.

And so did I—to look pretty and act sociable.

"Good morning," my perky voice would chirp over the phone. "This is Future Vista Enterprises. May I help you?"

I had fun, too. I dated some of the young executives...slightly older versions of the boys I'd dated in college. I slept with some of them. Had some decent, if unspectacular sex. I even got a proposal or two.

After all, men equated the qualifications of a good wife with those that made me a good receptionist. They didn't seem to want anything beyond a sunny disposition and a cute smile.

Oh, men liked me in bed, too. I didn't think that I was very spectacular, but I'd been raised to be sweet and play the role of the princess. So even when I didn't absolutely love it, I pretended that I did. Men liked that. Everyone would go home a winner. Sometimes I would, too.

And then came the contest. Some genius at the Bay Area Business(men's) League came up with the idea of the Miss Corporate California competition and sold the idea to the state organization. Soon it was being touted in companies throughout the Bay Area that this was the supreme opportunity for nubile young women to prove their ultimate worth in the business world.

All they had to do was parade in front of a panel of community leading lights in semiundress and respond to a lot of stupid questions.

The winner would receive prizes that a variety of enthusiastic businesses had contributed. Also there was money. Especially, there was money—ten thousand dollars of it, a car, a flight to anywhere in the United States, and a year's supply of canned fruit. The fruit, the flight, and the car were nice, but the ten thousand dollars was what I was after. We all have a price, and at the time, ten thousand dollars was mine.

The moment it was in my hands, I vowed, I would move out of my mother's house and into my own apartment, hovel though it might be. I would flip good old FVE the bird and study piano seriously again, and try to find places to play where audiences had an appreciation for real talent.

I'd already been at FVE for the better part of a year. To call it an ordeal wouldn't be accurate, but there were times when I began to suspect that if some bright light offered me a means of escape through matrimony at just the right moment, I might accept. I'd deal with the consequences of such impulsiveness later.

The contest seemed to be a better option. So, at the urging of several of my deskside oglers, I submitted my photo to the screening committee at FVE. Two weeks later I was informed that I had qualified for the competition.

That's how I found myself in a modest bathing suit, standing in front of the CEO and six other high-ranking company types. I felt completely naked. It was insecurity, perhaps. But the looks on their faces, to the man, told me that they saw me with no clothes on at all. They saw everything.

Maybe that's why our staff photographer couldn't come up with a single photo of me for the company newspaper in which I'd smiled. I won our company-wide preliminary anyway.

The Bay Area competition was conducted with all the pomp and ceremony of a Miss America pageant, complete with questions to demonstrate "intelligence" and personality. There was also a talent competition. This was in the era before such things were organized and run by pros, and most of the "talent" consisted of resurrected high school poetry recitals, baton twirling, and quasi-pop singers who learned their songs phonetically by listening to the record.

I figured I had it made.

I was moderately concerned about a busty, statuesque blonde. But her two-digit IQ was obviously a concern to the judges. While they personally couldn't have cared less about her ability to analyze *War and Peace*, they had to be worried about the corporate image of the region. It wouldn't do at all to send a bimbo to the state contest. Guess who that left? Yes, I blush to admit it—raven-tressed Elizabeth, a winner all the way.

The judges agreed.

It was worth the indignity, I told myself as I walked down the makeshift runway in the ballroom of the St. Francis Hotel. My most regal smile was glued to my face. If all went well, this would be my ticket out of the stupid corporation.

It didn't go quite as well as I'd hoped. At the state competition, blonde was the thing. The winner was a blue-eyed surfer type, a UCLA graduate who'd been a homecoming queen and later was the first runner-up in the California Miss USA or Miss America competition.

I finished a distant third and went home, happily invisible again. I quit FVE and rented myself a tiny, furnished apartment that allowed just enough room for a leased console piano. Mother insisted on giving me a little money to tide me over, fussing all the while about the way I was isolating myself now that I'd left work. She was especially worried that I wouldn't be meeting all the eligible young men of the corporate world.

What I couldn't tell her was that I was in the midst of a raging affair with the executive assistant to the CEO of one of the biggest corporations in the state. He'd been a judge at the state competition. Mother would have broken a blood vessel in her joy. Then she would have pressed me for details and marriage plans.

Unfortunately I could provide her with neither; details would have shocked her, and marriage plans were unlikely.

Daniel Harrington. Big Dan. The biggest jock on the block. That's what he had been at Cal, the hot-shot senior, football player, president of the best fraternity on campus. He could outdrink just about any man at a Friday beer bust. He pulled down a respectable 3.3 GPA, although he'd never be mistaken as a member of the intellectual set.

Nor did he want to be; it didn't suit his image. And image was the essence of Dan Harrington. He taught me a great deal about the power of illusion.

I was just a lowly freshman, even if I was a Kappa pledge. Dan never saw me. He was too busy playing up to the blondes with rich fathers. If it sounds as though I had a problem with blondes it's probably true. There was something about those all-American blue-eyed, light-haired creatures that always reeked of confidence. They knew what they wanted—the best sororities, the best men (by their standards), the best marriages, the Junior League, beautiful, bright children, a house in Pacific Heights, country club membership.

By and large they were a boring, predictable bunch.

24

But they knew how to get what they wanted. They didn't want to be concert pianists. They didn't worry that they weren't tall enough, that they didn't like to ski or play tennis. They didn't concern themselves that they might be the wrong kind of pretty. They were never afraid that if they wore their hair or makeup the wrong way they might not look as classy as they should.

They were the true princesses. And they were going to get the prince without kissing a single frog. Because it was their birthright, along with flaxen hair and fathers who didn't die in the war and came back to become doctors or lawyers or the heads of corporations.

Dan was blond, too. At six foot three he towered over most of his peers. His clean, healthy looks and broad shoulders marked him as a man among men, and catnip to women. Chosen for one of the most prestigious executive training programs in the country, he was already executive assistant to the CEO of Netweb Inc. and he was on his way to the top.

I realize I was an interlude. Maybe not even that. I was there and available. And pretty in the wrong way. I wasn't someone he would ever marry. But he could show me off and bed me until he was ready to select the mother of his future children. I was sure it would be someone who would never expect him to understand the music he heard at the concerts she dragged him to. But after all, she'd have to maintain her image with the other Symphony League ladies.

Honestly, he wasn't right for me, either. But a woman can know a man is absolutely wrong for her and still want to marry him, and most importantly, want him to want to marry her. How else could she be sure she was a princess unless a man wanted to marry her?

I could feel him watching me during the competition. He was the youngest judge on the panel. All of the girls in the contest had already spotted him. He was the topic of most of the backstage conversation when we weren't bitching about how the contest was a meat market.

I'm sure that he imagined me naked. Later he told me so. But this time the scales were balanced, because that's exactly how I saw him.

Things got interesting at the party in honor of the winner and the four runners-up. I hadn't seen anything in the rules that stated that beginning an affair with one of the judges after the pageant was over constituted grounds for disqualification. And I doubt if I would have cared if I had.

As one of the official belles of the ball, I danced with all of the judges, beginning with the president of the Bay Area Business League, who was pleasantly asexual and indifferent to my charms other than in an objective "we're pleased to have you representing us" sort of way. Nice man—bland, but nice. After him, I cut a rug with "Happy" O'Reilly, a local DJ who had just hit it big by winning a contract with one of the major rock stations in L.A.

"I voted for you all the way, baby," he said, as he held me too close and tried to grind his erection into me. I did my best to keep him at arm's length.

"Thank you," I said courteously, and heard the echo of my mother's voice. Mother, by the way, was in bed with the flu. So she didn't get to experience firsthand what I'm sure she anticipated would be the second-most important event in her little girl's life. Need I add that the most important would have something to do with wearing white in front of hundreds?

"Yeah, you've got real potential," O'Reilly said in

his booming radio announcer's voice. "You ever get to L.A., and you should, that's where it's happening, you call me."

"Oh, yes, I certainly will," I gushed, still smiling my beauty contestant's smile.

And then it was Dan's turn. As I suspected, he didn't remember me from Cal.

"But I'll never forget you again," he said in a low voice, holding me close. This time I settled into the protective enclosure of my partner's arms, wanting him to hold me this way in private.

"I can't believe I let you get away from me. But what can I say? I was just a dumb jock."

"Not so dumb," I said, looking up, way up, into his blue eyes, still sounding like the adoring freshman, hopelessly enamored with my football hero. "Look at what you've already accomplished. You'll be a CEO by the time you're forty. Everyone says so, even the business section of the *Chronicle*."

He laughed, a man's rich, rolling laugh. I just kept melting. "And we all know what the word of the *Chronicle* is worth. But who knows?" he shrugged. "They may be right. Forty is a long way away, and I may just make it. I'm sure going to give it my best try."

As I think back to it now, I cringe at the sheer banality of the conversation. But what difference does conversation make when the only thing two people are really thinking about is when and where they're going to tumble into bed together?

"I want to see you again." His voice was kind, but seductive.

"I'd like that." My reply came innocently, sweetly, but was just as seductive.

"It's not just that you're beautiful, you know. There's so much more that radiates from inside. Intelligence, a gentle, feminine quality."

Blushing, I could think of nothing to say. My head was swimming. Take me, I'm yours, every hormone was saying.

"I wish that I could take you out of here and home with me. Now."

"That's impossible," I said regretfully. "Everyone would know. And talk. We'd both look terrible." Mother's training prevailed after all. Even in the heat of the moment I'd recalled the overriding need to maintain appearances. Dan sighed. "Yes, of course, you're right. But when? When will I see you again? I have to see you."

"Yes, of course," I murmured. "But I can't tell you what to do. You tell me." He'd like that. Oh, big, strong man, make all the decisions. Leave me no responsibility for what may happen.

"I have a dinner meeting tomorrow night, but Thursday is open. Tell me where to pick you up. We'll find a quiet place where we can eat undisturbed."

"I live with my mother in the Marina. I'll write the address down for you. What time should I be ready?"

"Your mother?" He stopped dancing and held me away from him, a bemused expression on his face. "I didn't think anyone did that anymore."

"You do if you don't have enough money to do anything else." I tried to sound apologetic. "That's one of the reasons I entered this stupid contest, so that I could afford my own place."

His subtlety began to flag. "How soon are you moving?"

I laughed. "Does that mean we don't have a date the night after tomorrow?"

It would have been easy for him to back off then in response to my sarcasm. But, thank God, he laughed.

28

"Was I being that obvious?"

"Yes," I said shyly, looking away from those gorgeous blue eyes. "But it's okay. I understand." Then I looked back, directly at him, and laid my trap. "I want to have a lot more than dinner with you, too."

I could almost hear the jaws of the trap snap shut as Dan laughed again.

"You're wonderful," he said, pulling me closer. "We'll have dinner and talk about it. And maybe I can help you find an apartment."

"Oh, I'd really like that." I was lost. I wanted him to kiss me, and I didn't care who saw or what anybody thought.

We parted at the end of two dances when I was claimed by another of the judges. But not before I told him my address and phone number.

I went home that night in a state of anxiety, the oldest anxiety known to women—would he call?

Two days later, he called. We really had a dinner date. He would pick me up at eight. I was ready at 7:30, proud of myself that it wasn't even earlier. I put on a dinner suit. I was elegant, every inch the lady, not too exotic, a Kappa to the core. Not exactly a princess, but close. And I was ready for Dan.

He arrived promptly at eight. The sight that greeted my eyes at the door was awe inspiring. He wore slacks, a turtleneck sweater, and a sports jacket. Unfortunately, we were completely out of sartorial synch. Why hadn't I asked?

"You look beautiful," he said. And all wrong, I thought.

"Thank you," I responded. And then, "I should have asked where we were going. I'm way overdressed. It'll just take me a minute to change."

"Oh, that seems such a shame," he said, clearly relieved by the suggestion.

"No, no, it will just take a minute." And with her usual splendid timing, Mother charged from the kitchen to entertain Dan while I changed.

I rushed to my room, praying that she wouldn't get out the albums from the war filled with pictures of my father, or bore Dan with my childhood pictures. I hoped she wouldn't fawn all over him and scare him to death.

But then, he was probably used to it, I told myself. Big Dan was every mother's dream son-in-law.

Dinner. The restaurant was somewhere on the Richmond side of the park. A small neighborhood place, it was chic before we even knew how to pronounce the word.

It wasn't out of the way, in the sense that no one you knew would be there. In fact, we saw two couples of which the male halves were business associates of Dan's. Their presence slowed down our meal considerably. We couldn't be too obvious that we were rushing through the preliminaries of dinner before rushing off to the main course in the bedroom.

Dan's bedroom. Dan's apartment. The color scheme was mostly tan. It was decorated tastefully, but with a masculine edge, without being too macho. It was all very fashionable without being trendy...sort of *GQ*.

Of course, we weren't much interested in Dan's decorator sense. He led me to the bedroom without further ado.

We slowly undressed each other, caressing and kissing the ever-increasing amount of bare skin. We laid down on the bed, kissing and fondling. He nibbled on my lips, my throat, my breasts. Meanwhile, one of his hands had worked its way down my belly to my pussy. He teased my clit then ran his palm over the entire surface. I wanted to fuck him so badly I wasn't sure I could even finish the preliminaries.

"I want your cock inside me," I whispered huskily.

Instead of complying, he moved up and used his hands to lower my head toward his shaft. I could see he was leaking; pearly drops had formed at the tip of his penis. I licked them off and told Dan how delicious they tasted. I had to have more. I began pumping him and sucking until I sensed he was ready to come. I pulled my mouth away. "Fuck me. Fuck me now," I begged.

Smiling, he plunged his stiff rod into my pussy. His balls slapped against my skin as he moved his hips and penetrated to my very center. We both came quickly.

I gave him good reviews. He had some interest in my pleasure, but wasn't quiche-eating sensitive. Good enough to promise better things, especially once I had my own place and we didn't have my mother waiting up for my return.

It had been good enough. And it did get better. I fancied myself in love before very long.

That's what nice girls did, of course.

I was proud of my newfound studio apartment in Baja Pacific Heights. It was mine and I'd found it on my own. Dan had somehow forgotten his promise of assistance. In fact, he was out of town on business most of the time I was looking. I made it as homey as my limited resources allowed, using the best of early Cost Plus. The decor was probably too cute, and too cheap, and too feminine. But Dan made admiring noises when he saw it. Somehow, though, most nights after we'd gone through the motions of dinner, a movie, or a play, we'd end up back at his place, never mine. To him it only made sense. His place was so much roomier, and was perched on top of Nob Hill, complete with bay view. And that's what romance in San Francisco was supposed to be all about.

More importantly to Dan, we were on his territory.

We saw each other once, sometimes twice a week, when he was in town. I wanted to see him more, but I wasn't stupid enough, or secure enough, to tell him that.

Dan was the first man I'd ever known who wore silk underwear. He did it long before it was an acceptable thing to do, and it was the kind of thing only a man who was over six feet tall and had been captain of his college football team could do. He told me he'd started using them the summer after graduation. His first pair was a gift from a girlfriend who'd spent the summer in Paris. He confessed that he liked them so much he started ordering them himself from the little shop on Rue Royale.

I loved him in those silk briefs. They were blue, but not baby blue. Dan would never have been that precious. Midnight blue—deep, rich, midnight blue. Not bikinis, but fitting low on the hips, tight, sleek, and shiny over his exquisitely curved butt.

How I'd been enflamed when he was holding me close, wearing only those briefs. I liked nothing better than to feel his growing hardness through the thin material, then watch as the smooth circumcised cap rose blushingly above the elastic. By then my passion would be uncontrollable, and I'd almost tear the briefs from him and engulf his cock in my mouth.

I was leading an incredibly wasteful life. After losing the Miss Corporate California contest to the beautiful blonde from Beverly Hills, I didn't do much of anything except play the piano. I can't even call what I did practicing. I played without discipline or purpose. And I saw Dan. And I thought about Dan. That was my life.

My third place finish in the state final had brought me three thousand dollars and some jewelry and a few other things I didn't want. I sold most of it for a fraction of its value. Living off that money was easy while I lived for Dan, who lived for his career.

But, at least I was one up on my mother. I existed for a man who was still living.

About a month after the competition, I received a call from the state sponsors. While Bay Area folks had never been organized enough to make use of their "Queen" once they'd crowned her, the state crowd had different ideas. They determined that they wanted to use all five of the finalists for a variety of public appearances throughout the state. Dan, damn him, thought it was a great idea.

"It'll be good for you," he said over dinner one night. "You shouldn't just stay home all day...even if you do spend most of the time practicing the piano," anticipating my usual lie as to what I did with my time. "You need to get out, meet new people."

But you don't understand, I wanted to say. I didn't want to meet new people. I didn't need anyone in my life but him. I didn't need to do anything with my life but love him. Loving is what the women in my family did best. And loving him was all I wanted to do. He couldn't understand that. Or maybe he did and that was the problem.

I suspected, and then confirmed as true, that I wasn't the only ornament Dan used to impress people. I think that he cared about me more than others. But it suited his image to be playing the field.

So of course he thought it was a good idea for me to travel, to meet new people. It would get me out of his way, leave him free. It would free him of having a woman that was doing nothing else but loving him. This, even though he loved every minute of my loving him, just so long as he didn't have to do much in return. It still hurts to think about it. I sometimes surprise myself with the continuing depth of my vulnerability.

The pageant promoters had little training classes for us in L.A. in which we were taught the true meaning of the American dream, the gospel according to the almighty corporation. We were turned into custom painted and coiffed automatons ready to go out and preach the good word of our sponsor, mostly to men who were more interested in the shape of our legs and the size of our breasts, but also to women in the office. So what if they were chained to their typewriters? To them the message, I suppose, was that this was what they could aspire to—success, smiles, and sex appeal. Life didn't have to be an endless succession of days spent carrying coffee to the executive suite or taking dictation.

Mea culpa. Mea maxima culpa.

I was a Republican dupe.

While in L.A, I reencountered Hap, the DJ, during one of our little corporate-sponsored soirees. To his credit, and my relief, he gave me only a professional come-on. He was convinced that I could have a career in broadcasting. I wasn't so sure and the matter didn't progress beyond speculation.

For the next few months I travelled frequently. Dan was on the road as well. We saw each other once a week at most.

When we were together life was terrific, at least on the surface. I was riddled with anxiety about his sangfroid in regard to being away from me so much. His casual indifference to all the men I met, men who found me beautiful and desirable, often infuriated me and left me drained and insecure.

He didn't care. It occurred to me that it was an

34

extension of his own masculine vanity to have other men want me, but to be smugly confident that I would turn them away.

He was right, damn him. I didn't want anyone else. I couldn't even consider it. I don't know what I would have done if not for the call.

It came one night after I'd endured a particularly wrenching bout of Dan-inspired self-doubt. It was from Hap's program manager. The station was looking for a traffic girl, he told me. They wanted someone to go up in a helicopter at rush hour in the morning and evening and describe conditions on various freeways. Back then this was a new concept, and his station wanted to be quick to capitalize on it.

It sounded totally absurd to me, at least until he told me that the job paid twenty thousand dollars a year—a fortune considering my then state of affairs.

But why me? I had to ask. I had no experience in broadcasting.

They wanted a new face, he said, someone fresh.

A face? Wasn't this radio? Who was going to see the face behind the voice?

He laughed at my naiveté. Hadn't I heard of promotion? The plan was for a huge print, television, and billboard campaign, with the traffic girl's picture featured prominently. According to Hap, mine would make one hell of a picture.

They were interviewing twenty girls. If Hap's judgment was to be trusted, I would be a shoo-in.

I went to the audition. More posing, more posturing But two weeks later I was told I had the job.

Any normal, intelligent person would have been thrilled. But a woman obsessed generally is not normal, or intelligent, for often lengthy periods of time. I didn't say yes right away, but asked for a week to think it over. They wanted me and so, reluctantly, agreed.

I didn't tell Dan about it right away. I was afraid of his response. It was exactly what I expected.

"What a terrific opportunity," he enthused.

"But it means leaving you." How pathetic I sounded.

"I'm in L.A. at least once a month on business," he countered. "And there are always weekends. It's not as if you're going to the other end of the country. It's only an hour's flight. Besides, what are you going to do, stay here and play the piano all day after your year of Miss Corporate San Fransisco promotions run out?"

No, you jerk, I thought, I'm going to marry you and set up your house and give great parties and be a fabulous hostess and after a year or so get pregnant and have the first of our two perfect children.

"I've made some contacts to do a few recitals here," I offered feebly. "Only in churches, but it's a beginning. Maybe I can get a steady radio job here."

Dan snorted. "That kind of thing doesn't just become available, here or anywhere else. It's a one-in-a-million shot to have it handed to you like this. I don't see how you can do anything else but grab it."

"There is something else I could do," I said, knowing the words that were going to come out of my mouth. Well, what the hell, I thought, what did I have to lose?

Everything.

"I could be your wife."

He didn't seem surprised. Anticipating this moment, he must have prepared his speech months before.

"You're very special to me, Lizzie, but I'm not ready to get married. I don't think I'd be very good husband material right now. I'm so centered on my career. You wouldn't have much more of a life as my wife than you do now. You'd give everything and get so little." He even ran his fingers through his hair, trying to look despondent.

It all sounded so noble. And it translated into, "I'll never marry you. And it's getting too close and uncomfortable. Here's the solution to my problem." He had an out, a perfect out. I had this terrific opportunity. He could end the relationship without being a heel.

I'm proud to say I didn't cry. Not then. I mustered my pride and more or less agreed with him. I said I would take the job. Then I said good-bye. I didn't want to see him again before I left. He said he understood, but that if I changed my mind, I could call him.

"There won't be any need to call," I said calmly. "I'm going to L.A., and you can go to hell."

I'd loved and I'd lost. And I was going to L.A. to see what I could make of my life.

Chapter 3

Los Angeles—a city full of stars. Who would have thought that I'd be one of them? Okay, so I was only a small star in a minor galaxy. But when the lists from publicists for event openings went to the media, my name was usually on them. And I was just as likely to have a camera pointed in my direction as any starlet. Admittedly, the footage wasn't likely to be aired, unless it was taken by our sister TV station.

But as far as my mother was concerned, I was Elizabeth Taylor, Jane Fonda, and Sophia Loren in one glorious package. She was so proud of me that she even stopped sending clippings of the wedding announcements of the girls who had attended high school with me. In her own way, Mother was getting her consciousness raised.

A year after I left San Francisco, she also decided that since she was already this far away from me, she could tolerate an even greater separation. I almost died when she announced over the phone that she was going to sell the house in the Marina and go live with her sister in Florida.

Oddly enough, I was disturbed by this change in the

order of the universe. It would constitute a bona fide rite of passage for me. It wasn't that I felt any particular closeness to her. There'd always been a certain distance, no matter how much she'd invested in my life. Mother was a man's woman without a man, and wasn't at her best relating to another woman, even if it was her own daughter. She'd done her best, by her standards. Probably by everyone else's, too. And now her job was done. She was free, as free as she was capable of being. I felt happy for her. Weeks after the big move was over, I admitted I was relieved. At least I was free of the emotional shackles she'd bound me with.

I never quite unloaded my other emotional baggage—Dan Harrington. Big Dan and his midnight blue briefs.

Screw him, I told myself on more than one occasion. Only I kept wishing I could have. But he never called. And I'm proud to say I never did anything worse than hang up on his telephone answering machine. To this day, I'm convinced he did the same to mine. Modern technology opens so many new avenues in interpersonal relationships.

The next several years in L.A. were rewarding ones. I moved up to reporter, then was promoted to morning drive-time anchor, then advanced to a reporter's job at a local TV station. We weren't network affiliated, but in L.A. you didn't have to be to gain celebrity. I had a career. I had men. I had marriage proposals.

I had...nothing.

Yeah, yeah, I kept carrying that stupid torch. I look back now and I understand that life was a great deal easier that way. My therapist helped me to discover that it was a lot simpler to love someone in absentia than to adjust to the day-to-day complications of an ever-evolving relationship.

40

Mother, on the other hand, met and married a retired raincoat manufacturer six months after she moved to Florida; she's still living happily ever after.

I wallowed in self-pity the first year AD—After Dan—felt lessening melancholy the second year, and thought I was really over him by the third. Then one day, I read something about him in the *L.A. Times*—he was in town arranging a merger. He had advanced to the tier just below the upper executive level of Netweb. It reopened the wound just when I'd begun facing the world without my "Closed for Repairs" sign.

I might have been pathetic, but I still had my pride. I was Elizabeth Renard. I'd been written up in the entertainment columns. I knew men who could buy and sell Dan Harrington and not even bother to count the change. So why shouldn't I avail myself of my opportunities? I was ready. I'd show the men of Los Angeles a thing or two.

Of course I fell into a relationship even dumber than the one I'd endured with Dan.

I just wasn't very good at finding Mr. Right.

By the time I was ready to commit myself once again to the quagmire of love, I had worked my way into my current specialty, entertainment coverage. In L.A. that's a genuine accomplishment. It was frivolous, too, and arduous. Every day I'd have to deal with egos of celestial proportions, both in the newsroom and on the beat.

But the good thing about doing my kind of work was that even the worst of egos, when they're being interviewed, want to show their best side. Illusions. People outside the business continue to ask me if this celebrity or that one is as gracious in person as he or she is on screen.

I used to answer in the affirmative. Then it

dawned on me that these people were performers. Who the hell knew what they were really like?

What's more, I didn't care, just so long as I nailed down my story.

The year of my L.A. debacle began with a local scandal that was rife with interesting twists. No, there wasn't a murder involved. And it didn't involve a movie or television star. But it caught the romantic fancy, not only of the denizens of Smogville, but of the world...for the usual twenty minutes.

I covered some of it when it happened. And ten months later, I got caught in the aftermath.

Etienne St. Germain. He was in his early twenties at the time, I think. It was hard to be sure. Etienne was one of those Peter Pan-types who would look twenty-two when he turned forty-five, and probably have just about as much maturity. His features were black, his skin café au lait, his eyes blue, his hair a soft, golden brown, and curly.

I was never as impassioned with Etienne's hair as I was with Dan's ass, but I came close.

Then there was his voice—gentle, mellow, with a charming French accent that reinforced his continental aura. That voice was enticing at first, compelling so much of the time, cloying and annoying at the last.

According to Etienne, the story of his life was a great romantic tragedy. He seemed almost to revel in the sadness of it.

"My father was an American executive held in very high regard by his company. He was rewarded for his good work by being assigned the presidency of the Paris office. The women who was to be my mother, a black woman of extraordinary beauty, began as one of the secretaries in his office. They were drawn to each other almost from the start. Before long they were deeply in love."

This is, of course, an abbreviated version of the details. I'm not about to let Etienne become the central figure in my own drama.

"She left the company, for reasons known only to her and to my father. Their affair had remained discreet. A few months later, she and my father married.

"Their union put an end to further advancement in the company by my father. But the executive committee decided that firing him would cause too great a scandal. And after all, Paris was Paris. Wasn't it the birthplace of the romantic scandal?

"My father was very good at his job, but when clients came to France, the home office arranged whenever possible for them to meet with someone other than the division president. It was ludicrous how they made excuses for it. But my parents lived with the knowledge. That sort of nonsense is a trifle when a love between two people is so perfect.

Their greatest desire was to have a child. After three years and a difficult pregnancy, my mother gave birth to me. She wasn't healthy, and the doctors advised that she never have another.

"I was to be the ultimate symbol of their love. But this was not a simple thing. Even in Paris, I soon learned that I belonged nowhere. Not only because of my color, but because of my American father.

"I tried to prove that I was as French as anyone. I refused to speak English, even to my father, except when forced to in class. I tried to be like the other boys in my school. But I was never accepted.

"I resolved to stop trying to be. I remained apart. I withdrew more and more into myself. I felt alienated from everyone, even my parents. Between us there was love, but little understanding. Perhaps this was my fault; I cannot say.

"My one joy was music. I don't know what would

have become of my life had I been deprived of it. By the time I was five years old, I could sit at a piano and play any music I'd heard.

"My schoolmasters were impressed. Of course, my skill set me apart even more from others my age. But I didn't care. They decided to structure a special course of study that would allow me to emphasize music. They became convinced that one day I would play the world's great concert stages."

As it turned out, Etienne's goal wasn't quite met. He enjoyed a career in music, but it was closer, I think, to the one I would have had if I'd pursued my goals in the art. He performed in concerts and recitals, but almost exclusively in churches and colleges. He achieved some small degree of fame, playing with second-rate orchestras in Europe. He was good, but good in the way that a thousand similarly talented people are who might or might not rise to stardom.

He could have fostered a romantic image that might have taken him to the pinnacle, but Etienne would have none of that, or was incapable of it. Critics pointed out that there was a certain coldness in his playing that emanated from even the most passionately composed passages. His technique was flawless, but when it came to feeling, Etienne was always slightly removed.

That's also how he made love.

He reached the height of his career with an opportunity to play with the Los Angeles Philharmonic. His timing was perfect. It was low tide in the social season. And the ladies of the symphony's auxiliary took to him one after another, basking in the reflection of their vanity in his shining blue eyes.

Etienne was very adept at making those eyes shine and dance in response to the interest of the woman

44

before him. He was so very skilled it would take even smart, experienced women longer than it should have to penetrate the illusion and peer behind the mask.

There were, of course, ladies who didn't care, or who even preferred to live the illusion. One of them, as is often the case in such circles, had show business connections. She found Etienne a job as a musical consultant, whatever that is, with one of the studios. A suitable position was also created for him in her, um, heart.

"The ladies were so kind to me," Etienne would say. "I was flattered. But still I was empty. There were always women. I will not pretend that I don't know that they find me attractive. But what did I have when even the most skilled of them had left my bed?

"And then I met her. She was lovely, fragile, shy— not like the other ladies in Los Angeles who were so frightening in their cloak of brittle sophistication. She was many years older than I. But it didn't seem so when we were together. She had been married forever to a Philistine of a banker, and they had a daughter.

"But this woman was like a sweet, tender young virgin. She loved me in a way I had never known. Ah, to be loved so completely, so innocently.

"I met her at one of those ridiculous ladies' teas. It was in my honor, of course, and I did my duty. I smiled. I was kind to all of them. I kissed hands. I charmed. And then I met her. I was enchanted. I had to be with her."

He pursued her, seduced her, and for several months they basked in the flame of each other's passion in a series of discreet matinees at his beachfront apartment. Unfortunately for her, love for a woman was secondary to Etienne when it came to his career, even if he didn't quite like to admit it.

An important piece of music found its way into

Etienne's hands, and the lady, his fair Louisa, became just a little less significant, although I don't doubt he still loved her very much. It was a concerto, modern in texture, but with romantic overtones. It suited the state of his emotions. He was sure it would be a masterpiece, that if he could premiere it at one of his concerts it would ensure him fame and fortune.

"Louisa was so caring, wanting me to have my dream made real. I didn't ever imagine the lengths to which she would go. She had an inheritance separate from the money she'd appropriated from her husband's account. Without my knowledge, she went to New York and arranged a commission, not with the New York Philharmonic, for that couldn't be done. But the orchestra was talented and the hall was an important one. The critics who mattered would be there.

When I received an invitation to debut the work I was ecstatic. This was everything I'd hoped for. I didn't ask questions. Maybe in my heart I knew what my Louisa had done, but I didn't, wouldn't acknowledge it. I knew only that it would be a magnificent night. I would be hailed as a new and major talent.

"My highest expectations were exceeded. The composer got his credits as well, but he was all but forgotten. The glory was mine. I tried to remind people that I was only the communicator of his genius. But it was the concerto and Etienne St. Germain that captured the imagination of the press. Soon, to everyone, the music was known as 'Concerto for Etienne.'

"But the price of this fame was the curiosity it aroused. The music world is a gossip-filled community. It took little trouble to track down the secret of the commission. The world learned what I had not really wanted to know. I felt that I would be regard-

46

ed, and ridiculed, as a kept man. I loved Louisa for giving me my concert. And I hated her for making me look like a fool.

"Yes, I know it was cruel and stupid for me to think that way. But my mind was in conflict. I knew it was unlikely that I would have had the opportunity to play without her underwriting the concert. But now the triumph was forever removed, I thought, by the disgraceful position into which I had been placed.

"Then there was the added scandal of Louisa's subsequent divorce. I loved her. That didn't change. Nor did her love for me. She had given me so much, had ultimately surrendered her entire life. How could a man turn his back on that kind of love?

"I could not. And not for a moment believing that what I was doing was the right thing for either of us, I asked her to be my wife. She refused me. I admit now that I both was relieved and grateful. But she did agree to come with me to Europe."

What Etienne neglected to include in his melodrama was the fact that he was far from perceived as what he truly was—a man who had been, and would be, assisted in his livelihood by smitten women. Instead, he was portrayed by the media and perceived by a willing public as a romantic figure.

We loved it—our own modern-day Duke and Duchess of Windsor. All for love and that sort of thing. So romantic.

And so helpful to Etienne's career. Even though concert schedules in major halls are normally planned months and even years ahead, many were adjusted to include a special appearance by this new Valentino of the keyboard. There were radio and television appearances as well. He was the man...they were the couple...of the hour.

It was all so utterly compelling. But, as in so many

romances, the librettists of operas having it right, such romances only work out if one or the other or both are killed or separated in some dramatic way. That way the passion and our adoration can live on and we don't have to watch the laundry get dirty.

Etienne did well at first, so long as he stuck to "his" concerto. But that could only last for so long. Critics were soon pointing out that he was a one-note pianist. So even during Etienne's glory days there was specter of trouble on the horizon.

He had his world, in which, for a short while, he was celebrated. Louisa was shy, out of place, even more so since her life became subject to public scrutiny. He began socializing without her. For her there was loneliness, for him as much guilt as he could muster. The whole thing steadily came apart.

The lovers quarreled, privately and in public. Etienne's temperament became increasingly erratic as important critical and social circles were less and less impressed with his talents or his charms.

"It all became quite hopeless. We were so sad. We loved each other. A part of me will always love her. Our souls touched. That is not easily forgotten. But we could not go on together. She could not live in the world to which I belonged. Once she had given me a great gift, but now that gift became an anchor that would soon drown us both. She went to England where she had friends. I think she lives in London still."

He returned to the United States. There were enough small-scale engagements to keep him going, and enough ladies to pay him his due. He survived.

How he loved telling his tragic tale. It was difficult for me to refrain from diminishing it with the harsh light of probing questions. But even with what I knew and suspected as a hardened reporter and a woman full of cynicism and disbelief, I was touched. Well, not in the way Etienne usually touched other ladies. I never contributed to his financial support. But I did find him attractive in a strange sort of way.

I met him briefly when he first hit the public spotlight. I interviewed the "happy couple." He did most of the talking in an accent so thick I was inclined to doubt its authenticity. Later I learned it was real, just thickly layered and practiced. A man would be a fool to lose a French accent in the United States, especially in the presence of women.

At the time, Etienne was mostly just a story to me. The romance of it all, the passionate conflict, the apparent love, at least on the part of Louisa, aroused in me a passionate jealousy.

Dan Harrington would only had to have told me to "stay" and I would willingly have done it. Etienne and Louisa, in the beginning, had done everything for each other, for their love.

It practically killed me.

Once they had departed for Europe, the scandal was old news. But I never entirely got it out of my mind. When, months later, I met Etienne at a party, I immediately asked about Louisa. He looked wonderfully tragic and told me they were no longer together. I am ashamed to admit how many emotions and hormones he stirred in me with that one beautifully spoken line.

I mean, this guy was good. Later, much later, when I regained my sanity, I of course realized that the story of his lost love was as well practiced as his accent.

Later, over drinks on the patio of his apartment overlooking the Pacific Ocean, he told me his heartrending story in its entirety. My sole thought was to comfort him, to prove to him and to myself that love still existed, that the two of us could find happiness in each other. We made our best effort that same night.

He seemed passive, almost shy, as I removed his shirt and drew down his pants and shorts. He wasn't quite so passive as I thought; his cock was *hungry* where it hung pendulous and swollen.

I kissed his neck and chest, then moved downward. My hair brushed all around his loins as I maneuvered around my target. I touched the tip of his cock with my tongue and felt him shudder. I positioned my mouth to take all of him. Licking up and down the entire shaft, I varied my rhythm and intensity. I circled the head and swept down along the base. Etienne finally responded and pushed my head further down; his lance pricked the back of my throat.

He pulled back and positioned himself above me, putting my legs around his shoulders. With a single thrust he entered me, filling my pussy with his hard cock. His strokes were long and deep, coming faster and faster. His hands grabbed at my breasts, pinching the nipples, kneading the mounds. I felt him expand within me and I came at the same instant he did. He seemed to pump into me forever until he finished, then he slowly rolled off me. We fell asleep in each other's arms.

It was the beginning of our affair, although the pretense of love dissipated quickly. Still, being tenacious and not wanting to admit in my first post-Dan try at commitment that I'd made another huge mistake, I went on with it. I was faithful to him and functioned as a woman in love, without having the slightest illusion after the first weeks that he was in love with me. I needed someone in my life at that point, and I was willing to delude myself that Etienne was all I needed.

That he was never really there for me, that the emotional texture of our relationship evolved from his indulgence in his own sorrow, seeking my sympathy and warmth at the moments most convenient to him … I ignored these things and told myself that he would come around in time. One day his pain would be gone. And then he would love me entirely.

All right, so I still had some illusions.

But it didn't matter. Etienne was never what I really wanted. I knew this.

I would have this dream that I was marrying Etienne. But I could only see as far as the wedding, never beyond.

There I was, breathtakingly beautiful in my white gown. My dark hair and eyes contrasted starkly with the fabric. The only splash of color was provided by my lips—ruby red. Etienne and I would be standing in the receiving line, joyously accepting congratulations.

Suddenly, Dan would appear. He'd take my hand, wish me well, and then impulsively kiss me on the cheek. As he did it, I would whisper in his ear, "I'll always love you."

I really hated my subconscious.

Etienne and I endured. My work continued at a breakneck pace. His agent was able to get him engagements with minor orchestras in small cities, usually with the stipulation that "Concerto for Etienne" be in the program. He had recorded it during the first flush of fame and it had continued to sell. So he was able to maintain a modicum of self-respect.

Los Angeles, however, was Etienne's bane. Each time he appeared, the same second-string critic, Andrew Byrd, would tear him apart. Each review would be more vicious than the last.

We would both dread the day after an opening. We'd get the morning paper, anticipating the worst and not even coming close to the reality. No matter how Etienne prepared himself, he was always devastated. I was consumed by sympathy for him and could offer him no comfort that he would accept, no matter how he seemed to demand it. When, at last, he would submit to being consoled, he would come to me as the arms of a loving mother. For days afterward, no matter what my libido craved, there would be little chance of satisfaction.

You can't fuck Mommy.

Naturally, the subject of my musical abilities and the presence of the Baldwin baby grand in my flat were things we tried to ignore. I strongly suspect that if I'd stayed at it, I would have been better than Etienne. Never in the time I knew him did I ever play the piano in front of him. Nor did he want me to. I was sensible. I didn't want to be as good as I thought I was and confront him with it. Then I'd have to cope with whatever vanity required him to do to diminish my abilities in his mind. It was a losing proposition either way.

Oddly enough, the man I did play for, without fear or pretension, was Andrew Byrd.

My L.A. beat covered mostly Hollywoodish stuff—glitz and glamor, tits and tinsel. But from time to time, someone would remember my musical background and assign me to a story that related to it. Sometimes it was marginal, like the Etienne-Louisa story. But sometimes it was more serious. That's how I met Andrew, by covering a reception for a visiting ballet company.

Chapter 4

Having seen Andrew Byrd at performances around town, I recognized him immediately. Knowing my temper, I thought it would be best to ignore him or pretend ignorance of his presence. What would be the point of a confrontation, especially when lurking inside of me was a general agreement with his assessment of Etienne's limited abilities? Of course, that didn't excuse him for being a vicious bastard in print.

My luck was terrible, I groaned. He saw me and apparently knew who I was. He immediately came toward me.

"Whatever do you see in that never-was has-been?" was his opening line. Not bad. Andrew certainly knew how to make a strong first impression. But I was ready for him.

"What a surprise. You're just as nasty in person as you are in print. But not nearly as witty."

Need I say that this was a beginning that could only lead to one of two places—his or mine.

Mine.

He had a surprisingly large, firm cock. I made him lie down on the floor as I stood over him and removed my clothes. When I was naked, I made him watch me as I fingered my clit with one hand and fondled a nipple with the other. If it was possible, his erection grew even larger.

I stepped over him and lowered myself until my pussy lips met his mouth. He began to lick me. Being a sarcastic bastard wasn't the only thing he knew how to do well. He sucked on my clit for an indescribably long time as I bathed his face in my creamy juices.

When I tired of this, I reversed my position and licked my way down his chest and belly. I surrounded his cock with my lips and began to suck him off. When I figured he was going to lose control, I stood up once again, then lowered myself directly onto his pole. I fucked him by tightening my muscles around his penis, squeezing and relaxing, squeezing and relaxing, until his body started to shake. I raised myself off his cock so that I could see his great warm spurts erupting into the air.

In the morning, for some masochistic reason, I chose to play the piano for him. I suppose I had to prove to him the extent of my fearlessness. His response nearly floored me.

"If I were reviewing the entertainments, both of this morning, and if you'll forgive me, of the night before, which latter review I'll refrain from making because to do so would be a decidedly ungentlemanly thing to do, I would be tempted to say this: that after a stunning climax to what seemed to be the final aspect of the performance, this reviewer was delightfully surprised to discover yet another aspect of the young lady's apparently endless store of versatility and appeal. You really are quite a good musician. You shouldn't have been so quick to surrender your hopes for a career. If you'd kept at it you would have far surpassed your French friend.

My shock changed to elation. "Do you actually think I'm good, or are you just saying so to strike yet another blow at poor Etienne while pandering to my ego?"

I, too, could speak as if every brilliant word was waiting to be etched in stone for rediscovery at some later date.

"You wound me. I do think you're extremely talented. And you have feelings you aren't afraid to risk in your music. That's far more than your pet piano player is willing to do." He stood behind me, running his hands along my shoulders, then over my breasts. "Tell me, honestly, isn't he a bit of a passionless bore in bed?"

"I won't tell you anything," I sniffed indignantly, "any more than I would tell him what kind of lover you are."

"No, I don't suppose that you *would* tell him that I had been so presumptuous as to trespass into your boudoir and dared to caress your glorious flesh. I should think that would be our little secret."

"Are you thinking of telling him?" I couldn't believe what I was hearing. "Is that what this is all about, another blow you can strike at Etienne? Surely, even you wouldn't be that despicable."

"Come on," he said as he walked away, stopping before the window. "Let's be honest. You're a beautiful woman. We both know that. If I had seen you at the reception and known nothing at all about you, I would still have wanted you. But can't you also admit that a part of your participation in last evening's activities was related to the assumption of how devastating it would be to *cher* Etienne if he found out what we were doing? You've taken pleasure in knowing that you've just been fucked by his worst enemy. That attitude is so female."

55

"And you are a total bastard. That's so male."

"Bravo!" he applauded. "You've wounded me. And, to make it so much the worse, you've done it by turning my own phrase. I'm impressed, even as much as you intended me to be. And excited, more than you can imagine. Let's go back to bed."

The man was like something out of a Noel Coward parody. And I have to admit I adored him more with each passing minute. Passion was clearly secondary to repartee as far as he was concerned, but I didn't care. With Andrew, I could virtually have a mental orgasm. If I was going to mind-fuck, he was certainly the ideal partner.

For several weeks, I alternated sleeping with both of them. Two nights a week I spent with Etienne in his beach apartment. One or two nights Andrew arrived with a flourish at my flat. Somehow, I felt safer with him on my own territory.

How he intrigued me. At that point, he was certainly a hell of a lot more fun then Etienne, who was spending increasing amounts of time enthralled with his own personal tragedy.

One man so tedious. The other so amusing.

I kept thinking that it would be much more honest of me to end my relationship with Etienne. But whenever I got close to doing it, he'd start telling me how much he needed me. Plus, the truth was that having both men were becoming increasingly necessary to me.

But only if I had them both.

Was it the beginning of perversity in me, or just the first notable outward manifestation that I was steadily progressing toward some great psychological revelation?

One night as Andrew and I were talking in bed, he said, "You know, I've never actually met yesterday's boy wonder. Wouldn't it be interesting if you introduced us?"

"It would be horrible," I retorted. "How could I do that to him? And why would I want to give you the opportunity to attack him to his face and probably tell him about us? How can you ask me to be a party to such cruelty?"

"Because cruelty is the farthest thing from my mind. I promise to be exceedingly charming and kind. I already feel much more gently disposed toward the lad than I have in the past. You have softened me."

"Somehow I hadn't thought that was the effect I have on you at all."

"Much too obvious a riposte, my dear. Definitely beneath your abilities."

"And of course, you prefer me beneath your abilities."

He waved his hands in mock surrender. "Enough, enough. One more double entendre and I shall have to attack you in retaliation."

"In print, or to my face or some other portion of my anatomy?"

"Bitch. You're trying to provoke me to your whorehouse level of repartee, but I shall neither stoop nor rise to the challenge."

But, of course, he did.

With the initial assault out of the way, Andrew began a campaign to meet Etienne. The subject dominated our conversations. I began to feel that it didn't really matter which one of them I was with, at least conversationally. Either way, we always wound up talking about Etienne.

And then my little demon of perversity elbowed me in the ribs again. Go ahead. Do it, the little voice urged. You know the very idea makes you wet.

I agreed to it, but only if we could make the meeting look accidental and if Andrew agreed that he would say nothing to Etienne about us.

About a month later, Andrew and I were invited to the same cocktail party and I agreed to bring Etienne. I couldn't resist anymore. I was dreaming of the two of them every night. I had always been fairly conventional in bed, although I'd been told I was a good lover. No illusion there; I'd always been easily carried away by pure, delicious lust. And as evidenced by my response to Etienne and his tale of woe, I could be terrifically caring and protective of the male ego. Mom would have been proud if she could have seen her little princess.

One of the things that intrigued me about Andrew was that I never did or was required to do any of the typical things with him. If we played the roles of bastard and bitch, at least we were equals. I fed his vanity with real delight at his wit and wickedness, doing my best to top him when I could. Sometimes I succeeded, although he was loath to acknowledge it.

I don't suppose that was the healthiest basis for a relationship. I didn't think so even then. But I was enjoying it. I left the analysis to my analyst, whom I was seeing less and less of as I saw Andrew more and more.

If Andrew was bringing out the darker side of my nature, then so be it. Obviously, it was something that was meant to happen. He was only the means of my deliverance.

Etienne and I arrived at the party before Andrew. How like him, I thought, to make me wait, anxious, on edge, wondering if he would come or not.

When he finally made his grand entrance, he flashed me a smile that said, "I knew you'd be waiting." Bastard, I thought. He read my expression, smiling with that conceit that was uniquely his. If there had been another exit, I would have ushered Etienne out of there immediately just to thwart the bastard and his evil intent.

No. I guess I wouldn't have.

I could feel the muscles in my face altering my own expression. I met Andrew's smile with my own. Oh, it was all so rotten. So far I had told Etienne only that I had met Andrew at another event and spoken to him briefly. He wanted to know if I'd given him hell. I told him that I had not. To do so would not only have been unprofessional, it would probably have hurt his career even further.

"What more could he do to me?" Etienne whined, falling prey to what I thought was his most annoying mood. His agent had been coming up with fewer and fewer bookings of consequence. Despite this, I noted that Etienne not only succeeded in getting his rent paid, but each time I went to his apartment some significant new article of clothing or piece of jewelry had been added to his substantial collection. I suspected those were rewards and tokens of appreciation from ladies of greater means and less reluctance than yours truly.

I'm not saying that Etienne took money for his somewhat limited prowess in bed. At least he didn't take it directly. That would have made him a prostitute and would have horrified him beyond words. No, he was content to accept payment for being a sort of dancing bear of the keyboard, playing the piano at parties, ostensibly as a guest, the hostess pleading with him ever so gently to tickle the ivories, and then hers, for just a little while.

With a great show of reluctance, he would graciously acquiesce, the illusion of propriety preserved in his mind and the lady's. Ego once again protected from reality, he could accept his trinkets.

As to his prowess in bed with me...the sad truth was that my morose maestro was less and less competent as time passed. My interest waned as well. But I felt sorry for him and did my best to comfort him.

I remained willing to hold and caress him on long, sleepless nights, and I didn't want to desert him.

But the whole affair was depressing me and was taking its toll on my work. I found myself perpetually tired, worn out by the constant wringing of my emotions and the lack of sleep and my warring feelings for Andrew and Etienne.

Andrew, thank goodness, rattled my cage. He challenged and stimulated me. I looked to him to the restore my psyche and to deliver me from Etienne. No, I couldn't leave him when he so clearly needed me. But, as I'm sure my subconscious was aware, I could drive him away by doing something truly horrible—such as bedding Andrew Byrd and making sure that he found out about it.

Andrew circled us like some cautious hunting cat, prolonging his approach by stopping to talk to several groups who blocked his path. Etienne was so engrossed in conversation with a lady who was eventually to become yet another of his benefactresses, that he wasn't even aware of Andrew's presence.

I could hear my heart pounding, feel my adrenalin flowing. I had never been so thoroughly aroused as I was at that moment with the smell of confrontation in my nostrils.

Andrew, when he greeted us at last, oozed snake oil salesman's charm. He was every bit as fascinating as the serpent in Eden. Only this time, it was Adam he was trying to tempt.

Etienne didn't know what to do. Prepared to dole

out righteous anger, he was taken off-guard by Andrew's casual friendliness. Andrew didn't even allude to the spate of unfavorable reviews he'd written over the years. Instead, he talked generally about the music scene, asking Etienne for his opinions, listening politely, respectfully, to his responses.

Before Etienne knew what was happening, he was snared. He had fallen under Andrew's spell, completely forgetting, at least for that moment, that this man was responsible for many of his woes.

If there's one thing more powerful than the vanity of a man, it's the vanity of a male musician. All resentment was lost, all suspicion was suspended as Andrew courted Etienne with simple flattery. Initially I thought it was to goad him on to even greater displays of ego and foolishness, which Andrew would later turn against him. I was wrong...and incredibly naive.

Within an hour, the three of us—best friends—left the party in search of a place to dine.

It was in the restaurant that Andrew began his courtship in earnest. I call it that, because courtship was most certainly what it was. Lip smacking, lascivious, obvious courtship. It hurt to think that two men in my life were more interested in each other than they were in me. But even in that I was mistaken.

I was more confused than anything else. Andrew and Etienne displayed unbridled passion for me in bed, actually surpassing anything we'd experienced previously. I struggled with the nagging belief that our relationship had become an exercise in sublimation. I wrestled with the thought that I was, for the moment, the closest they could come to bedding each other.

That coupling grew out of a tripling.

One night the three of us attended a very bad concert. Our eloquent trashing of the soloist reached new heights as we sipped cognac in front of the fire in Andrew's living room. It was terrifically cozy. We were all feeling the glow of the liquor, growing ever more enamored with our collective wit.

That's when Andrew looked at Etienne and said, not so cleverly, I thought at the moment, "The man is a passionless dolt."

There was one of those horrible, prolonged stretches of silence. It probably lasted only a matter of seconds, but the web of camaraderie that had been woven between us could almost be heard to snap.

"Are you talking about me?" Etienne said in a menacing voice, every blistering review clearly as fresh and festering as it had been before the meeting with Andrew.

And, I thought, Etienne, to whom I'd given little credit for vast intelligence, had perhaps not been Andrew's dupe at all. It was possible that he'd gone along with all of this to await the proper moment for his revenge.

I eyed the poker resting by the fireplace, wondering if I was about to become witness to a murder. The tension was palpable.

They were sitting in tan leather chairs, facing each other like gunfighters preparing for a showdown. Andrew reached across the figurative and physical breach and put his hand on Etienne's arm.

"Oh, no, dear boy. I was very wrong about you. I know that since we've become friends. I suspected that your greatness lay just beneath the surface, and wanted to goad you into becoming the artist that you were meant to be. In my glib cruelty, I failed. But now I know that your passion is there, ever present, waiting to be released, to become ecstasy."

The air was thick with lust, enveloping not only

the two of them, but me as well. I was the link. Without me, what was growing between them could not be consummated. I had been used, but my usefulness gave me a certain power.

Even after we'd become a social threesome, none of us had ever discussed what transpired behind bedroom doors. Andrew and Etienne both must have known that I'd divided myself between them, but that unspoken knowledge seemed only to add fuel to our passions.

In bed Andrew was motivated by a creative as much as a physical drive, and yes, by vanity. And although he wasn't a handsome man, he was attractive enough in an academic sort of way. He was tall, on the lean side, greying at the temples, slightly myopic, and wore horn-rimmed glasses. He was so bright, so clever. And he intrigued me.

Andrew especially had risen to heights of extraordinary excitement.

Etienne, on the other hand, had always fucked by rote. Sometimes he was as mechanical as he was on the piano. But he was strong and athletic and technically very accomplished. Interestingly, his self-pity had largely evaporated during the formation of our social trinity, and his charm, although often cloying, had once again predominated. I was sure he knew that I had taken Andrew as my lover. It seemed to have created a spirit of competition.

I would willingly accept the consequences.

I could see an erection straining the fabric of Andrew's trousers. The excitement was palpable, almost physically painful for me. I wanted both of them. And as much as they might have wanted me, they wanted each other. I was the catalyst, the force that would propel the inevitable.

I entered into my role, an utter slave to my raging

desire. Rationality was forgotten. I knew what I wanted with frightening clarity of vision.

Wordlessly, I moved from the sofa. I sat on the floor between them and began stroking their legs, gently, using just the slightest touch. I didn't look at either of them.

In a moment, first Andrew and then Etienne brushed my arms with their fingertips. I looked first at one and then at the other. They were smiling.

In a moment, we were all laughing.

Andrew, who of course had to be the leader, stood up first and pulled me to my feet. Etienne followed. There was a brief pause, a final opportunity to regain sanity.

The moment passed. None of us felt the slightest hesitation.

Andrew's bedroom was an adolescent fantasy made real. The first time I'd been admitted to the inner sanctum I'd laughed out loud. Andrew had been so offended we almost never made it to the fur-covered, king-sized, satin-sheeted water bed. My whispered apology and a husky promise to make it up to him appeased his wounded pride, but thereafter I made every effort to sleep with Andrew in my more conservative surroundings.

This night, though, tackiness was the last thing on my mind.

I don't know quite how to explain the feelings I experienced. They weren't so much different from the moods that overtook me when I got screwed by Andrew or Etienne alone. But, perhaps, with the addition of another penis, everything increases proportionately.

I was probably the only one of us who retained a flicker of rational facility. It was probably the reporter in me. It kept me just slightly removed from the action so that I could observe, make mental notes, form phrases I could use later when it was time to describe the abyss of passion into which I'd fallen.

But, oh, I was so close to shutting down my faculties that night. Added to animal passion was the stimulation of exploration into a sexual domain where I had never been nor ever expected to be.

This was all before the AIDS epidemic, and I was of a generation that regarded sexual freedom as an inalienable right. But even then, such a step was foreign, forbidden.

Thrilling.

We came together, at first wordlessly, and began slowly undressing each other. We showed remarkable restraint, I thought, considering the heat of the situation. But that made it so much more exciting.

Nonetheless, this being real life, not a well-choreographed film, there were moments when awkwardness would overtake us, when we weren't quite sure what or whom to reach for first.

But that became a part of the joy. We laughed as our efforts became more frenzied and hilarious. We were like innocent children playing with their first sexual discovery.

At one point, they both went at me as if I were some kind of inanimate, life-sized doll that had just been given to them for Christmas. I loved it. I stood still, moving an arm or leg only as they moved me. It was winter and layered clothes were fashionable. Even in warm Southern California, wool sweaters and boots suited the elements.

They pulled off my cardigan, and then my turtleneck sweater. Then Andrew unhooked my bra, while Etienne slid it off from the front. My nipples, hardened and raised, beckoned to them. They responded readily, sucking at my tits. I moaned as they tugged with their teeth and ran their tongues over my sensitized skin. I felt like a mother who had just given birth to aberrant twins.

Their shirts were off by then. Etienne had his pants unzipped and they had begun to slip down his legs, making him look slightly ludicrous. Andrew was the most dressed, the most composed of the three of us. His pants were still closed; his belt was even yet to be undone.

How like him, I thought, in a fleeting fragment of thought. It kept him in control to the last. I reached for his belt buckle and loosened it in two swift movements. Then I opened the fly of his slacks, pulling them down to his knees so that he looked totally absurd.

I laughed uproariously at the sight of the two of them.

Retaliation was immediate.

They went at me as if I were a rag doll, pulling and tugging. I began to fear I'd be dragged about the room, a victim of childrens' carelessness.

Their actions weren't violent or hostile, though— just silly and so sexy.

They halted their mock attack of me long enough to remove their dangling trousers. They were free now. Wearing only their briefs, they came at me anew.

Etienne, the larger and stronger of the two, lifted me up under the arms, swinging me off the ground, while Andrew pulled off my skirt and burgundy satin slip. A lace G-string, knit black panty hose, and black leather boots were all that remained of my ensemble.

Etienne returned me to my feet. I stood there as they circled me.

"Isn't she pretty?" Andrew said, just within reach, touching me ever so slightly on the nipple of my right breast.

"Yes," said Etienne, "*tres charmante*." He moved in just a little closer and brushed the inside of my leg.

"I think I like this best of all," said Andrew with a glancing touch to the area around my pubic hair.

Around and around they went, coming just a fraction of an inch nearer with each rotation, commenting on my body as if it were a thing independent of personality, touching me just barely, but with increasing intimacy.

I stood motionless, as if I were indeed a thing, a physical thing, bereft of will or intelligence.

Then, without further preamble, Etienne was in front of me, Andrew behind. Etienne caressed my inner thighs with his hands. Andrew massaged, no, *kneaded*, my buttocks, as if they were two rounded loaves of bread he couldn't wait to bake, then consume.

Jointly, they pulled off my panty hose and boots, flinging them to the side. Then, like a pair of groping schoolboys, they reached inside my panties. Their fingers began probing my pussy, separating the folds, darting in and out like single-minded snakes. I gasped, barely able to stand under the assault.

They stopped only long enough to remove their own briefs. They tore off my G-string, then lifted me into the air like a captive sacrificial virgin ready to be flung into a volcano.

They flung me onto the bed, surrounding me on either side. Hands, lips, tongues, touched me everywhere.

And then, because I was merely the appetizer, they went from me to each other. Reaching across my prone body they embraced, kissed, deeper, deeper, their mouths locked together.

I was fascinated.

Repulsed.

Aroused.

Jealous.

They separated, their hands reaching for the other's penis, fondling, stoking. I couldn't tear my eyes away from the sight of their stiffening cocks. They appeared larger than I'd ever seen them and they hung, throbbing in anticipation of what was to come.

Then, as if set off by some internal signal, Etienne climbed on top of me. Just as quickly, Andrew crawled behind and mounted him. Etienne groaned at the violation, but the expression on his face was one of ecstasy. I barely saw the angry purple head of his cock before he rammed his entire length into me.

I was engulfed, crushed by the weight of the two of them.

I was also excited beyond anything I could ever have imagined.

Our bodies moved as one entity, thrusting, undulating. Etienne plunged into me with pistonlike regularity in response to Andrew's motion, then drew back as the pressure eased in his anal canal. I was sure it must have been painful for him, but he uttered no complaint as he pounded harder into my frothing cave. I was rocked by one wave of pleasure after another.

There was no way to prolong beyond that moment the union that we shared. Within seconds, we all came screaming our joy to each other and to anyone else who could hear us.

We separated wordlessly, each of us falling into a deep sleep that didn't end until nearly noon the next day.

Always one to insist on the last word, Andrew woke me while Etienne still slumbered. Despite my sleepy protests, he insisted that I fellate him, and wouldn't give up until I relented and let him ejaculate in my mouth.

How quickly extraordinary things became the norm. Our little ménage à trois continued for several weeks, each time becoming a little less interesting than the last—for me, anyway. Our configurations varied only slightly from that of the first night. The preliminaries became increasingly predictable.

I suppose, for the sake of the illusion of virtue, I should say I ultimately put a stop to it because I was disgusted by such perversion, that I realized how disgusting and sinful it all was.

But I would be lying. I left because I got bored. I left because the novelty of seeing Andrew's prick penetrate Etienne's asshole became stale pretty quickly. I left because of the knowledge that they were far more enchanted with each other than they were with me. Now I wasn't so enamored of either of them that I cared overmuch about that. But since I no longer had my libido or my ego gratified by the situation, it made it nonsensical to continue.

I had become nothing more than a minor, and probably unnecessary, catalyst.

I gave them little. I got from them even less.

I wasn't angry, but I did prefer to leave them to themselves. When I told them how I felt, they made obligatory motions urging me to continue the relationship. But in truth, I think they were both relieved that I was withdrawing.

It was all so terribly civilized.

When I left them I consoled myself by coming to the conclusion that neither of them would have filled Dan's midnight blue briefs.

No, romance just wasn't my strong suit.

But I contrived to excel at other things, reporting among them. The trouble is, skill doesn't always mean much in my business. Ratings, age, the wrong look, a major mistake, or a new news director who just plain doesn't like you can leave you suddenly out in the cold.

Guess what?

Our network was sold and I was too closely identified with the previous regime. Teacher's pet, that's how my new boss was heard to refer to me. What a shithead. It was only a matter of time until I got the old heave-ho. Of course, when the handwriting is on the wall you hope you'll have the balls to say "take this job and shove it."

But we rarely get those satisfactions. Besides, I was ready to move on.

The difficult thing is that once you're in L.A., where do you go? Everywhere other than New York is a step backward. But I didn't care about that when I heard about the opening at KSRK-TV in San Francisco. Home.

I sent my audition tape. I said my prayers. I played out the string at work, hating it more and more each day.

As for a sex life, it was only a vague memory of the recent past. Even San Francisco couldn't be worse.

Ha!

Four interviews later I got the job.

I was going home. Oh, lord, I was going home.

Men in San Francisco: they're either gay, married, or both. Or they're among the minority who are single and straight, and they're neurotic and spoiled and consumed with delusions of sexuality.

Sublimation is a major activity in San Francisco. Health clubs make a fortune from it. I've never been even remotely athletic. I once gave aerobics a shot, but I couldn't bear the sight of all those sweaty bodies in designer leotards and leg warmers. I was scared to death that I might become one of them. But I had to do something to fit in and to stay fit.

Although eventually I would find a more secluded cottage in another part of town, I began my renewed residence in San Francisco in an overpriced apartment in the Marina. I even had a view of the bay, but I had to stand on the toilet and gaze wistfully out the bathroom window to see it.

I was, however, close to the Marina Green, prime running territory. My shift at the station was from three to eleven, so I could run at times when most of the city wasn't doing the same thing.

After the first few weeks of straining muscles I hadn't previously known existed, I started to enjoy the exertion. It was during my fifth week at it that I had a revelation about runners' motivation.

At precisely three and three-tenths miles, I had an orgasm.

Considering it was the only kind I'd had in months, it wasn't so bad, especially since there didn't seem much hope that I'd reach one through more conventional methods.

Professionally, things went well. I was a general assignment reporter. As the new talent on the block, I didn't exactly draw the best stories, or salary. And I was the first one called in for overtime or asked to work weekends.

That doesn't imply I received all the rotten assignments. For instance, I arrived one morning and was told to prepare immediately for a hot interview.

"It's with Dan Harrington," my editor told me.

I froze for what I thought was an unnoticeable second. Then I stammered, "Who's Dan Harrington?"

"There's nothing like a reporter who knows the territory," the bastard replied. "Harrington is the president of Future Vista Enterprises. He's in the midst of a big feud with the town's most radical women's libbers. Looks like the broads may have won. He's called a press conference in his office— thirty minutes. And we're going to give the broads what they really want—television coverage. Get your ass over there."

"When the 'broads' finish there, why don't I just bring them over here to have a little chat with you?"

"Don't even try, sweetheart," he frowned. "You couldn't raise my consciousness with a crane."

For once I was glad he was such a jerk. It took my mind off the interview.

In the van, I tried to pull myself together. I kept telling myself I could handle it. I had to. San Francisco was a village. I was lucky I'd avoided him since my return. I'd tried to avoid thinking about him by ignoring the business section of the newspapers. Those weren't normally the kinds of stories I was assigned to anyway. But now he had to go and make news. It was just like him to do that to me.

I realized, though, that our meeting would be on my terms. After all, I was a hot-to-trot television reporter.

For all I knew, he might not have any effect on me at all. I had been a kid when we were involved. I was stupid, romantic, ready to be in love and ready to be hurt. I'd been unsophisticated, inexperienced.

I sure as hell wasn't any of those things now.

Silly me. When I saw him I wanted him just as I always had. I had to live with the realization that I was just as much in love with him as I had been on the day I left San Francisco. And I hated him just as much for letting me go.

I wanted him to love me.

And I wanted him dead.

The room was full of reporters and demonstrators. At first I stayed toward the back; I sent my cameraman up front. I watched Dan, tried to pay attention to what he was saying. Fortunately, I had a cassette recorder with me. Using it was the only way I could be sure that I would have any knowledge of what was happening beyond the interpretation of my own tortured mind and senses. Plus, if I wanted to add to my agony, I could play the tape back later. I could listen to his voice for hours, letting the sound of it and the memories of him fill all the empty spaces inside me.

He delivered his prepared statement. It started out with all of the expected information, statistics that he said verified that FVE was on a par with other companies when it came to hiring and advancing women to executive positions.

Actually, nobody had accused FVE of blatant discrimination. His company had been chosen as an example of San Francisco corporations. Also, Dan's increasingly high profile in the community upped the potential for media attention. As it turned out, the libber's strategy hadn't been a bad one.

"We're not in a position," Dan said, "to make any radical changes." There was slight hissing from the assemblage. But his gorgeous, all-American smile, perfect—probably capped—teeth, began to win them over.

His eyes were just as blue, his hair, just as blond and thick. The not-too-obvious designer suit fit just right; the shirt and tie were perfectly coordinated.

His expression was so open, so sincere. He came off as such a nice guy.

He was hiring management consultants, he explained, one of them a prominent equal rights advocate, to analyze the situation. He was more than eager to be fair, but he wasn't going to be bullied into anything. When, and if, he felt a major change in hiring practices was called for, he would institute those changes.

It wasn't much of a statement. There wasn't any reason for the pressure to stop except that he'd hired the right consultant. For the moment, there was nothing the feminists could do, not until he had the consultants' reports and had responded to them.

It meant, damn him, that the story would be ongoing. Now that it had been handed to me, I was required to follow up until the issue was resolved.

Dan said he was ready to take questions. I had a few, but said nothing.

The reporter standing next to me shouted something. I didn't hear it; I didn't care. But for the first time Dan saw me. He started to answer absently, then asked to have the question repeated.

I still didn't hear it, or his answer. He stumbled over it. That's all I noted. I was pleased at the effect I'd had on him—it was one small step for Elizabeth Renard.

It made me feel stronger.

He answered the next few questions with difficulty, looking at me every chance he got. I tried to keep my face expressionless, professionally objective. In a short time he recovered. He answered the rest of the questions with more control, more authority, more like Dan.

Then someone asked him why he was going to such lengths to solve the problem, if problem there was. He smiled that "Look, Ma! No cavities!" smile again.

"I know I have to say this very carefully, so that I'm not accused of being an even worse male chauvinist than I undoubtedly am. The fact is, I've always had a lot of strong women influencing me, even if they played more traditional roles. My mother, my sister, my wife—they've all impressed upon me that I had to be as fair as I possibly could in my approach to this situation."

Wife.

Wife.

WIFE.

The word resounded, it bounced around the inside of my head like a rubber ball.

The bastard had gotten married. Stupid me. I'd pictured him as an eternal bachelor who would commit to no one. That way my ego would have nothing to fear.

He was married. Christ.

The press conference ended. I tried to pull myself together, round up my cameraman, and get the hell out of there. A loose acquaintance, another reporter, asked me a question. I mumbled something in response and moved away quickly.

But I didn't move fast enough. My cameraman was already part of the way out the door when Dan came up to me. "You go ahead," I told the cameraman, trying my best to sound calm. "I'll be there in a minute."

There were still a few other people in the room, but it was clearing rapidly. Within a few moments, we were alone.

"You're the reporter from KSRK," Dan said, as if I were just a face he'd seen on a television screen. Maybe to him that was all I'd become. He'd made no attempt to contact me. I wondered what it had been like for him to see me on his TV all this time.

"I thought you people were supposed to be famous for asking the toughest questions in local broadcasting. You never said a word during the whole press conference."

I hated him. He was so sure of himself, so sure of me. It could have been days, not years, since we'd been with each other.

Yeah, he was a bastard. I hated him with such a glowing passion. I hated him for not being able to love me enough to make a life together. I hated him for using me. That's all it had ever been. He thought I was beautiful. He wanted to make love to a beauty queen, to have me as one of the ladies he showed off at corporate events. And his ego had been flattered because I'd been so obviously in love with him.

I hated him for every lonely night in Los Angeles, for the orgasms I couldn't have with Hollywood actors, for my whole sordid involvement with Etienne and Andrew.

I especially hated him for marrying someone else and for remaining the best-looking man I'd ever seen. He was still everything I'd ever wanted.

"All right, Mr. Harrington," I said. "I have some questions to ask. Are you going to give me an exclusive interview?"

"Of course," he said, confidently. "But you're on your own. Don't bring your cameraman back."

"Let's get started," I said, turning on the tape recorder.

I told myself that I was being a good, tough reporter. But when I played the tape back later, I heard only anger and hostility. And pain. There was nothing I could use on the air.

So, you'll use it for background, the reporter in me argued. That's what I told my cameraman I was doing when he came back to look for me. "Take the film back to the station." I instructed him. "I'll catch a cab when I'm finished."

When he'd gone, Dan asked, "When did you get to be such a red-hot feminist? You never seemed to care about any of that when I knew you."

"I didn't know any better. I've learned a lot since those days.

"Do your liberated sisters know that your career was launched by showing off some of your best attributes to a bunch of male chauvinist pig judges in a second-rate beauty contest?"

"Actually," I replied coldly, "I've never been able to convince the station to drop it from my bio, so it's common knowledge. We all do some pretty foolish things before we smarten up."

He reached over and turned off my tape recorder. "Foolish things," he said, "like having an affair with someone like me?"

"I can think of a stronger word than 'foolish' to describe that particular involvement."

"That won't be necessary. I get the idea. If you'll forgive an MCP comment, you still look terrific. You're more sophisticated, a little unnerving around the edges, almost a little too sharp, too savvy. But that's attractive, too. Youthful innocence isn't everything."

He moved closer to me. I tried to move away from him. I couldn't move in any direction.

"Why don't we just go someplace, have a drink, and talk," he said, trying to take my hand. "We have a lot to catch up on."

That made me mobile.

"Dan," I said, as I stood up, "do you remember what I told you the last time we were together, before I left for L.A.?"

"Yes, you told me to go to hell."

"Good, I don't need to repeat myself. The interview is over. I've got to get back to the station. I have work to do."

"When did you start to get bitchy?"

"Not bitchy. Just smarter and more self-protective. I learned from my mistakes, especially my biggest one."

Still so sure of himself, he tried to put his arms around me. Mine responded reflexively, stopping just short of lashing out at him. I, who had never made a violent gesture in my life, wanted to hit him as hard as I could.

It shocked him as much as it did me. He moved back quickly.

Loftily, I said, "I only let married men touch me after I've seen a written note of permission from their wives. Good-bye, Mr. Harrington."

I made a superb exit, sweeping from the room, never looking back.

My grand gesture was complete, my heart just as broken as it had always been.

I functioned adequately at work. It was only during the hours when I wasn't busy, especially when I tried to sleep, that the pain and anger overcame all else. I all but stopped sleeping. Whenever my head hit the pillow, my mind provided instant replays of our recent meeting, and of all the times we'd been together in the past. I also spent a great many early morning hours rehearsing hundreds of variations of the conversation I would have with him during our next inevitable encounter.

Several weeks went by. Then I read a news release handed to me by the assignment editor. Dan Harrington and the leaders of the city's most important feminist organizations were holding a joint news conference.

I was assigned to cover it and attended the conference with some trepidation.

"For the past several weeks," Dan opened, "I've been reevaluating my position on this situation. I've read the reports and the consultants' recommendations. Not all of them were in agreement. My first inclination was to proceed with the more moderate of the proposals. Thanks to the efforts of these ladies…sorry, of these *people*," he gestured to the feminist leaders, "and their fantastic abilities to organize the troops, I've been deluged with calls. I've been shown a brilliant display of womanpower in action and why it should be tapped even further to benefit our company.

"Being the stubborn type, along with my other negative traits, I admit all of this might have gone unheeded. However," cameras flashed as his smile penetrated the shadows in the room, "when my own mother suggested that I start going somewhere else for Sunday dinner, I felt that the time had definitely come for me to alter my stand on the issue.

"Therefore, I'm pleased to announce that beginning today, my top executives and I will begin work on a plan of action outlined in the strongest of the reports. This plan will establish specific affirmative action guidelines and timetables, which we believe will serve as a model for major companies throughout the Bay Area."

There was laughter, cheers, applause.

In defeat, he was the victor. He was charming. He was disarming. Villain no more, he'd turned the whole thing into a love-in with himself the object of all affections.

When it was over, I started for the door with my cameraman and the rest of the crowd. I didn't intend to risk being the last to leave. But as always, when Dan was involved, I had little control over my own actions. He caught me lightly by the arm, led me aside.

Quietly, looking deeply into my eyes, he said, "I did it for you."

"Were you always a liar," I asked, "or is that something new?"

Before he could answer, I pulled loose of his hold and walked out the door.

Three weeks passed. The story was old news. I began to recover. I hoped, halfheartedly, that I'd heard the last of Dan.

He called me at the station. He didn't identify himself, just started talking.

What conceit, I thought, as I listened to him babble. He assumed that I would recognize his voice. Well, I hadn't, at first. That gave me some satisfaction.

"I want to see you," he said, "just for a drink or lunch. We can eat in a noisy, public place, where everyone can see us and know that it's perfectly innocent. And so will you. We need to talk. This is a very small town and we're going to keep seeing each other whether we like it or not. Why don't we try to make it as painless as possible?"

I wasn't sure that anything that had to do with Dan Harrington could be painless. Nevertheless, I agreed to lunch. I even had myself convinced that he was right, that it would be better to get everything out in the open and then go on from there.

We were to meet on the following Monday. I looked at it as just a slightly more interesting way to begin the week. I'd handle it and maybe purge myself in the process.

After all, I wasn't some stupid girl in love with a man of greater importance and experience. I was somebody in my own right. I was an experienced woman who had known sexual adventures that Dan Harrington, Mr. Superstraight, couldn't have begun to imagine. I could have taught him a few things. If I deigned to sleep with him again it would be on my terms. It would depend on my mood and how much time I could spare.

My affair with him hadn't been all that momentous. Dan was just a typical slice of white bread, very bland. He was a middle-American corporate executive who'd been lucky enough to make it to the top of his little world ahead of most everyone else.

So what?

Even his midnight blue briefs were kind of corny now. I discovered later that he still wore them. I thought that after all the intervening years he'd have the imagination to try something new.

Then I jumped back into the quagmire. Why not use him for occasional stud service? I thought. He was good enough for that. We didn't live in the Dark Ages. Lots of women had affairs with married men, especially busy women who didn't want the emotional clutter that single men would bring into their lives. He wouldn't be the most important thing in my life. He would merely fill a biological need until someone better came along.

What a dope I was. Three years later I was still sleeping with him.

Chapter 5

At least I wasn't faithful to him.

It was pathetic—that the only point of pride I had in a relationship was that I wasn't faithful to my married lover.

And with whom had I been unfaithful? He was a picture-pretty flake of an anchorman who meant no more to me than I did to him. But I was able to take him out in public and see to it that we were mentioned in Herb Caen's gossip column from time to time. It kept people from snooping into my private life because they thought I was having a newsroom romance.

Dan and I were terrifically discreet. Naturally, a part of whatever pleasure we derived from the situation stemmed from the belief that we were getting away with something. There we were, two public figures, one of us married, and we'd carried on an illicit relationship that no one uncovered.

Of course it is possible no one cared. After all, it wasn't as if I were Alexandra Minette. While reading her autobiography I'd fairly salivated with envy. Now there was a woman who had known how to live.

She'd been famous, or as she insisted when I interviewed her, infamous, as an artist of pornographic portraits. Her affairs were legendary.

When I interviewed her, she'd gone back to her real name, Alexandra Rinsky, and she'd founded a quasi-religious international organization that, until I interviewed her, I'd been convinced was a joke.

She'd had romantic exploits with men most of us couldn't even imagine meeting. Among them was a libidinous Texas millionaire, a British lord, a Moroccan chieftain, and the king of a small country. Her memoirs read like a cornucopia of creative copulation. Not every situation had worked out well, but she'd always been in control of her destiny. My greatest desire at the time was to be able to say the same.

Mostly, Alexandra had used pseudonyms for her lovers, but there weren't enough kings of small countries left to enable that personality the anonymity he would have preferred.

"Yes," she'd laughed when I interviewed her. "It did cause poor Teddy [King Theodore of Latnesoria] a bit of grief with his kids. But they were used to his ways. His was one of those arranged royal marriages. The queen stuck around long enough to produce a son and heir and a couple of backups, then took off for the Riviera where she still lives happily ever after. Teddy continues to live it up just about everywhere. He probably would have liked it had I been a bit more discreet about things, but I'm convinced the randy old bastard quite loves the notoriety. We're still terribly good friends."

"Not lovers?"

"No, I don't have lovers anymore," she replied.

"Yes, I read that in your release. But what about your organization. Is it a spoof, as some critics have implied?"

84

"Absolutely not. I'm engaged in a very serious crusade. For now, I'm using the profits from the sale of my book to fund its operations. I do expect that before long membership and other contributions will finance it. There's no elaborate administrative process. Primarily, it's a matter of printing and arranging for speakers to spread the word."

"Would you say that it's like a new religion?"

"I don't think of it that way, although there's a certain gospel to it and it did come to me as a sort of revelation."

"Would you explain for our viewers?"

"Well," Alexandra continued, warming to the task, "it was a few months after I'd finished writing my memoirs. That was a very difficult period for me. There was an earlier draft than the one that was eventually published. I was quite despondent at the time. I thought of the manuscript as rather a long suicide note.

"But when I'd finished, I couldn't help but consider what a splendid life I'd had. On the other hand, what I'd been wasn't right for me now. And I didn't know what it was I wanted to do instead.

"Artistically, I'd stretched as far as I could, at least in terms of what was saleable. I didn't want to go on doing what I'd been doing, even if my artistic pornography had gone on selling as well as it once had.

"At the risk of sounding unduly crude, I had begun to feel quite strongly that once you'd drawn one penis, you'd drawn them all. It certainly seemed to me that I had, in more ways than one. So there I was, at this impasse.

"I was growing quite cynical about men. I suppose I still am. I mean, they are dear little things in their way, just so long as you don't take them seriously as people. Unfortunately, it was a mistake I kept repeating. The disappointment was shattering. I thought I was invulnerable to all the emotions that betray most women. I was forced to learn that I wasn't.

"Now, the romantics would say that's a good thing. It meant I had a heart. But if it's a thing that's just there to be broken, then what's so splendid about that?

"As for sexual adventures, I'd had more in reality than most people conceive in their wildest fantasies. But you can't spend your whole life going from one fabulous man to the next. Even that has an element of tedium to it.

"So I was at loss. I was spending a great deal of my time asking adolescent sort of questions about the meaning of it all, most particularly of my own life. I felt that I must be meant to do something important, but I didn't have a clue as to what it was.

"Then, one morning, as I was drying my hair, a bizarre thought rushed into my head like a gift from the heavens. I decided that this was the only kind of blow job I wanted to give from now on. I resolved at that moment that sex was a thing of the past for me. The more I considered it, the more sense it made. It became a kind of philosophy, a credo, if you will.

"For a long time I stayed in isolation. When I emerged, I knew that I wanted to found an organization. I would call it 'The International Say No to Sex Crusade.' I was convinced then, as I am now, that we should join together to conquer the ramifications of careless fornication. What the world needed was a return to wholesome values. If there must be sex, then let it be in marriage."

At that point I'd begun to think dear old Alexandra had a few loose screws rattling around in the attic. There was no stopping her.

"What had my life of debauchery brought me in the end? I experienced depression, regret, doubt, suicidal tendencies. How different it might all have been had I only known the evil source of the confusion that exists in all relationships. Sex. The desire for sex. The acquisition of sex.

"Even in marriage, it may be time to consider this an antiquated activity." She banged the table. "I'd like to see funding for more sophisticated methods of artificial insemination. I'd like to see the advertising and the entertainment industry stop glorifying sex. Put it in its proper perspective. If people weren't constantly bombarded with artificial sexual stimuli, with the illusion of the need for sex, they'd stop craving something that isn't very good for them, that confuses the meaning of life and human relationships, that's a transitory pleasure at best. Now it's even become the cause of a plague.

"Have I founded a religion? Maybe. But it has nothing to do with some sort of god figure, but rather the elevation of the human spirit when it is finally removed from the basest instincts of the flesh."

"Do you actually have members in this organization?" I asked sweetly.

"Oh, yes, hundreds. Soon it will be thousands."

"But your book directly contradicts what you're now advocating. It's the story of a woman who's had a wonderful life, who's lived out every possible fantasy. Why would anyone who's read your book be inspired to follow your current direction?"

"My dear," she said patting my hand, "would you really want to live the kind of life I had?"

"God, yes!"

"Oh, you have so much to learn."

"Exactly," I agreed, completely forgetting that the camera was rolling. "You wrote the perfect textbook."

Fortunately, she'd been more alert than I and graciously ended our chat before I could stick my foot further down my throat. "If you think you have enough for your interview, I'd be happy to speak with you while your crew packs up."

"Thank you," I said gratefully, considering what my last comment would do for the boys in the editing room. But I was lucky that day. I had a cameraman who liked me and there was a woman on duty in the editing room. As the cameraman carried the equipment to the car, Alexandra and I talked.

"You're a beautiful young woman. There must be so much in your life that's fulfilling. You're bright. You have a successful career. Why would you look at my life, my former life, as something desirable?"

"Because you had and did everything."

"I had everything but values," she corrected me. "I did everything but give meaning to my life. Now I have both. I hope you will some day as well."

"But you were in control of your life. I never feel that I am."

"I was a slave to my hormones. Now I own my body and my soul."

I wished I'd never interviewed her. It was all a fraud, I told myself. She still looked like the stacked redhead on the book jacket, but her hair was in a smooth bob now, and a suit jacket did its best to obscure her shape. It disconcerted me that every once in a while, though she'd tried to suppress it, there'd been a demon sparkle in her eye. Her crusade had to be a joke, I kept telling myself.

I regained my composure. "You've been a fascinating interview," I said. "Thank you. I wish you luck."

"Thank you. And I wish you well in whatever you're seeking."

88

I turned back to her just before I left her suite at the Clift.

"I'm curious about just one thing. I hope you don't mind my asking." I took her silence as assent. "The pianist you had that disappointing affair with. Was it Etienne St. Germain?"

"Why, yes. But how did you know? I barely referred to him and I deliberately didn't describe him physically because he was so distinctive. Do you know him?"

"I used to. Slightly. I was a reporter in L.A. and I did a story on him once."

"Really? I don't imagine it was very exciting. I don't think he was a very interesting or very happy man. Life didn't seem to be very successful for him. He didn't seem to be much admired by his peers or by the critics."

"I think he did get along with some of them," I said impishly.

"Really? How very nice. You see, there's hope for all of us. And I'm sure you'll find the right path to walk. Good-bye."

I couldn't wait to talk about her to Dan. We were supposed to get together later that night. He had meetings through dinner. We were going to meet at my place when he finished.

I never asked him what his wife said when he didn't get home until two or three in the morning. I didn't ask Dan any questions about his marriage. I didn't want to know anything. It was all so completely separate from me. I knew that, for the sake of my sanity, I had to keep it that way.

I didn't believe a word of what Alexandra Rinsky had said about her new life. Oh, I believed that she believed it, like one of those born-again Christians. But there was no way a woman who had lived her life for sex was going to give it up. Somewhere within her, Alexandra Minette still lived. Perhaps she only slept, awaiting the opportunity to emerge and reign once more.

Somewhere within me must be a similar spirit, I speculated. There was another, more exciting woman inside Elizabeth Renard. A woman who was waiting to be freed.

Dan and I had long ago gotten past the illicit excitement of our liaisons. We might as well have been married for all that was new and adventurous in the bedroom. Dan was a good, competent lover. His body continued to be a beautiful thing to behold. His penis especially was a thing of delight—thick and straight and almost imbued with a life all its own. It was a lance any knight worth his spurs would have been proud to bear.

Unfortunately, Dan had little imagination. And though I flattered myself that I had far more, I was fearful of crushing his male vanity by advising him on how to liven up our lovemaking. I didn't even consider introducing anything new.

It wasn't fair, I thought. If I was only to have him for a few hours a week, I at least wanted the best of him sexually. I wanted excitement, adventure. I wanted to be, deserved to be, Alexandra Minette. She was preaching the wrong gospel. If she couldn't see that she'd always been privy to the truth, I could.

When Dan arrived the night following my interview with Alexandra, I could barely get him to listen to what I was saying. He was so full of his stupid Business League meeting. I suppose he was entitled to be excited. He'd just been elected president. If you have a provincial view of things, I suppose that's a terribly important accomplishment. "Good for you," I told him, managing to make it sound sincere, even enthusiastic. Who cares? I wanted to say. There are more exciting things in life than bourgeois little men's club elections.

It was boring, boring, boring.

"But I don't want to talk about business—not your business, not my business. I want to talk about sex. I want to talk about lively, exciting, provocative, uninhibited illicit sex."

He laughed and teased me as I pouted. I was cute when I pouted, and it always worked with men like Dan. They thought it was adorable. It made them feel strong and powerful that I was such a cute little bit of a silly thing.

That part of it wasn't boring. It was appalling.

Daddy just loved his darling, pouting little girl. After all, he could always give her a new toy to play with to cheer her up. It was so much easier than coping with real grown-up emotion.

"You want to talk about something sexy?" he asked. "How about helping me plan some wicked entertainment for the initiation of the new Business League board members? That ought to give that lascivious little mind of yours something intriguing to occupy it."

I snorted. "What could possibly be lascivious or intriguing about that dreary annual banquet in some hotel ballroom with all those pathetic pompous men sitting around stuffing their faces?"

"That's the inauguration. The initiation is something else entirely. Private. Very discreet. In fact, I shouldn't even be talking about it. But you seem like such an unhappy little girl tonight that I want to cheer you up. Besides, I trust you, just as you trust me."

Dan was so full of it. What he meant was that we had so much on each other that we had to trust that neither one of us would endanger ourselves by betraying the other. It would be a mess for our reputations and our careers.

"So tell me all about it." I conceded. Not that I believed for one second that anything about that tedious group could ever be remotely sexy.

"What do you do? Something really daring like having a girl jump out of a cake?"

"They did that last year," Dan said seriously. "Then the new members took turns frosting her—and then licking her off."

"That's repellent. I don't believe you."

"It's absolutely true. Every year it's up to the president to come up with something new and stimulating for the evening's entertainment. You want to do something sexy, help me come up with something that will go down in the secret annals of the Business League as an all-time great."

I couldn't believe it. "You want me to help you plan some stupid, sophomoric stag party? Is that what the big, important business leaders in this community do with their energy? No wonder you people are in such trouble and half the corporations in San Francisco are moving out."

"Don't be fatuous," he chided. "You know this has nothing to do with it. Don't you think things like this go on in other cities? You're not naive. Why pretend to be?"

I took his arm. "Now let me see if I understand this. Every year the first responsibility of the newly elected president of the League is to come up with a live porno show to entertain his fellow pillars of the community. Why not just hire a gaggle of hookers and spread them around?"

"That's what we did two years ago."

The feminist in me—yes, there's a feminist in

me—told me to put an end to Dan's puerile stupidity. I should have responded with appropriate moral outrage and thrown the the bum out. The lurking voluptuary in me, however—the woman who would be Alexandra—demanded erotic creativity.

What emerged was the perfect concept.

"Look, Tarzan. Business is a jungle," I said. "So why not create a jungle environment, complete with setting, sounds, and the exotic creatures who populate such places? I'm sure you've got the imagination to understand that the animals would be of the feminine variety?"

Saying that, I curled my back like a wild cat about to attack. Thank you Minette. That idea had been in Chapter Five.

Dan flipped for the idea and was so excited at the prospects, he wasted little time before flipping me onto my back. Our lovemaking was almost bestial that night.

He was the king of the jungle.

We spent the first ten minutes locked in hard, wet kisses while he expertly fingered my throbbing cunt. Then, with an animal-like grunt, he lifted my legs over his powerful shoulders and plunged his cock into me. I watched as his perfect ass pumped up and down. We fucked for well over an hour, going through so many positions that I think I lost track. The whole time Dan wildly shoved his rod in and out of me. I'd meet each of his thrusts with raised hips, driving against him until I could feel his pubic bone against mine.

When he'd tired of the pounding he'd given me, I took his tired cock in my mouth and began to work on it with single-minded lip-and-tongue action. It took Dan longer to get erect this time, but when he came it was with major impact. His fluids nearly choked me, but I was able to recover and swallow every drop.

Later, we planned an evening the Bay Area Business League would never forget.

Nor would Dan Harrington.

It was to take place in the home of one of the wealthiest board members. He had a huge house, not in the obvious Pacific Heights or Hillsborough area, but in the hills of Berkeley—a forest environment surrounding a jungle interior.

Nice.

Of course, my role in all of this was a secret. I could only advise Dan. He and his minions—those who could be trusted with so important and confidential an assignment—carried out my instructions. They made the arrangements to hire the dancers who, in their elaborate makeup and translucent body stockings, would simulate tigers, leopards, and panthers.

The day before the big event I was able to persuade Dan to show me the house. He had a key; the owner was out. By that time the knowledge that the whole thing had been my idea had been completely erased from his memory banks. Naturally, he was more than delighted to show off the product of his brilliance.

There was some staff around, but they didn't pay much attention to us. Besides, the way I'd dressed that day—hair pulled back, nondesigner clothes, little makeup, tinted glasses—I was hardly recognizable as Elizabeth Renard. If anyone bothered to pay any attention to me at all, they probably assumed I was some mouse-burger secretary.

It was a setting that would have befitted a major charity benefit for the city's elite. No expense had been spared in decorating the ballroom. It was a jungle worthy of a Hollywood extravaganza—a lush, verdant, but benign rain forest, complete with a campsite and tables set for fifty or so "hunters."

How absurd they looked in their Brooks Brothers suits the night of the big event. They weren't prepared for what was to come. They were the pillars of the business community and completely out of their element. They looked ridiculous and wary, even as they salivated, imagining the possibilities. They were pigs.

It was clear that their uneasiness added to Dan's pleasure. He was the only one aware of what was to come. Even the owner of the house had only a vague notion. Yes, that gave Dan satisfaction. What men wouldn't do to obtain a sense of power. It must have resembled fraternity idiots who loved living in the past.

After a few strong doses of rum drinks and a meal served by "native boys,"—leaving the guests to wonder when the obvious topless "native girls" would arrive on the scene—they all relaxed completely. The only tension was sexual.

By dessert—some elaborate bakery concoction with bananas and more rum as its major ingredients—jackets had long been removed, ties had been loosened or displaced.

The sounds of pulsating jungle drums, cawing birds, and roaring lions mingled and escalated. Someone killed the lights. When they were restored, fourteen felines, one for each of the new board members, huddled on the floor.

There was another—a tigress for Dan Harrington.

Then it was the lions of industry who roared in approval of what they were about to tame.

At first the felines just danced, mostly with movements that could be seen on any disco floor. But in those negligible costumes, with no dance partners to distract from the impact, the effect was quite different. The dancing continued for about fifteen minutes. It was individual and free-form, except for the finale when each of the fourteen cats padded over to the new board member to whom she'd been assigned.

The execs were identified by the white safari hats they'd been ordered to wear just prior to the appearance of the dancers.

I knew Dan's curiosity would be piqued by the one feline apart from the others. It was my special surprise. Call it a special guest appearance.

While the rest of my pride lured their partners onto the dance floor, I continued to spin and gyrate and be ever more suggestive. I was almost intoxicated by the illusion I'd created, by the feeling of power that had descended on me.

The music reverberated from the walls. The movement of the bodies on the dance floor almost synchronized in its frenzied thrusting and grinding. The old boys gathered round to watch the fun, cheering, calling out the names of their associates, urging them to more daring activity than loose dancing and minor league fondling. Cries of "fuck her" were common from the tongues of these pillars of the community.

The dancing was to have been the big finish to the evening. The ladies were to divide their attentions among all of the attendees, until everyone had drunk enough and groped enough. Then all the pathetic bastards could return home to kiss their wives and kids and pretend nothing had happened. Half of them would probably jerk off.

I'd made a slight adjustment to the plan.

I moved to the middle of the floor and began to draw couples away, soundlessly steering them back to the "campsite" that surrounded the clearing.

Soon, everyone was at the sidelines. I swayed seductively to the edge of the floor and collared an amazed Dan Harrington. My claws—stage gloves sharpened to piercing points—grabbed his arms and pulled him to the center of the makeshift dance floor.

At first he wasn't sure what it was all about, but then he recognized me. And like a good little lamb he followed.

I began dancing with him.

"Bitch," he said under his breath so that no one else could hear him.

"Wrong animal," I responded. "You'd better do something to me soon, at least a little tit fondling and ass grabbing, or your image among your associates will be ruined forever."

It's amazing what a slight challenge to the male ego will do.

"If that's the way you want it." He lifted me up, holding me with one strong arm against my back. His other hand found its way to the crotch of my tiger's skin, rubbing fiercely and pressing against it. His mouth seized first one of my barely concealed breasts and then the other.

A cheer went up at first. Then there was an uneasy silence as Dan set me down on the floor and began fondling, no, attacking me.

For a moment it was all just close choreography. Then lust took hold of us, and in the midst of the crowd, we were alone. We were animals in a jungle we'd created together.

"Holy shit!" somebody whispered, the voice carrying strangely over the music.

I used my claws to rip Dan's expensive silk shirt to shreds. The tips went through the broadcloth to his skin. When I pulled them back there was blood under the tips.

He was magnificent to behold—so big, so commanding. He was fierce with anger and desire.

I brought the claws to my mouth, tasting his blood. Then I reached for the material of my body stocking, determined to break open my covering, to have him right there. My breasts were already exposed, Dan's lips working at them single-mindedly.

With the sound of the ripping material came the sound of a collective gasp from everyone in the room.

Suddenly, I knew where I was and what I was doing. I was about to let myself be screwed in front of half the business community of San Francisco.

I had never planned on being more than one of the dancers—anonymous. It would have been a good joke, to hear Dan's version of the party and then tell him that I had been there all along.

I had never anticipated the madness that possessed me, that possessed him. When he recovered from the passion of the moment he would be furious, enraged that I had put us both in so much jeopardy.

I ran from the ballroom, down the stairs to the lounge where the dancers had left their street clothes. I threw on my long coat and dashed, sobbing, to my car. Once inside, I tore off the rest of the costume and threw it in a trash can on Market Street. I wiped off as much of the makeup as I could, driving home with my smeared face, completely naked under my Ralph Lauren polo coat.

I shook with terror at what we might have done, with the knowledge of the primal things of which we were capable—that we might have been so consumed by them that we would have forgotten the consequences of our actions.

It had been what I wanted—to be like Alexandra, free to live sexually.

But the price. My career. My status in the world. Maybe I couldn't follow in Alexandra's footsteps. She was an artist, outside of the normal order of things. Her art and her life had been one. I could have destroyed my future. And for what?

For passion, I told myself. For true, all-encompassing passion. Passion that had become my most important need. Passion that had very nearly consumed me and consumed Dan Harrington.

What if I hadn't run away? What might we have done?

As I lay tossing in my bed early the next morning, I knew the answer.

Nothing.

Dan would have stopped. He would have risked nothing more in front of those men, his peers, his admirers. How he perceived his status among them would have stopped him. Maybe he knew what he had been doing all along. That would have been just like him.

He would have gone just far enough, maybe even stripping me naked before his associates. He would have done just enough to prove that he was a man who could take a woman if he chose to do so. But he would have stopped short of actually dropping his pants and whipping out his cock. Rutting in front of his peers or having the whole affair break down into an uncontrolled orgy wasn't in Dan Harrington's behavioral code. He would never have taken me in front of those men. He wouldn't have left himself so vulnerable.

But would he ever forgive me for tempting him, for leading him to the brink? I feared he would despise me, not only for what I had done, but for potentially exposing some weakness in him. Would he despise me because he might have lost control?

Or because he never could have?

If it was to be the end of our relationship, I knew I would be better off. I would be free of him and his machinations. I would be rid of his posturing and his domination.

For three weeks I agonized, replaying the night over and over in my mind. I plunged myself into my work. I took more than my usual load of assignments, did the stories and remembered nothing when the filming and editing were done.

When I could think, I thought of nothing but him. When I could feel, I felt nothing but him inside of me. I saw him, saw us as we were that night. But I saw us with no sudden ending to what might have been. I envisioned myself ripping off the rest of his clothes and the rest of my costume. I saw us proclaim ourselves before those men and those anonymous women as absolute lovers, as passion united.

I dreaded his call as I waited anxiously for the phone to ring.

I rehearsed what I would say.

No, I planned on hanging up the second I heard his voice.

I was a pathetic mess.

His call came at home the following Wednesday afternoon, just before I left for work. His voice was calm, matter of fact, commanding.

He gave me an address in Mill Valley and told me to meet him there at midnight. He didn't give me an opportunity to speak. When he finished giving me his instructions, he hung up.

I told myself that I wouldn't go. What could he possibly have had in mind?

I didn't want to know. I didn't want to risk knowing.

I knew I'd be insane to walk into such a situation.

Besides, I was peeved that he thought he could order me to appear and that I would jump at such a command.

The hell with him; I would show him who was actually in control when the time arrived. I wasn't going to give him the satisfaction of seeing me show up.

I threw away, with a flourish of triumphant self-assurance, the paper on which I'd written the address.

But I'd already memorized it.

The address was a house, deceptively rustic, not unlike many residences in the Marin hills. They looked like cabins, but they had everything from Cuisinarts to hot tubs. It belonged to friends of his who were out of town. They'd loaned it to Dan for those times when he needed to make a quick getaway from the city.

He was charm personified when I arrived, the perfect host. Flames flickered in the fireplace, the wine—my favorite chardonnay—was already chilled.

He didn't say anything about the jungle event. Actually, he didn't say much of anything.

We drank the wine, sitting close together on the oversized, multicushioned living room sofa. The atmosphere was heady and more than a little confusing. When Dan began to kiss me, I had a feeble show of resistance, then became completely responsive. Everything was going to be just fine, I thought, as he began to undress me. He hadn't been angry at all. It had excited him.

But why, then, had he waited so long to call? I pondered.

"There's something in the bedroom for you," he said. "To coin a very old phrase, I thought that you might want to slip into something more comfortable. Why don't you do that? And then I'll join you."

"All right," I said, wearily. Dan wasn't the sort for surprises. I didn't know what to expect, but I went into the bedroom anyway.

Dan knew I would. Just as he knew I would come to the house.

On the bed was a complete outfit, in my size. It was a costume for someone masquerading as a little girl. There was a frilly pink dress, hair ribbons, a little girl heart-shaped locket, Mary Jane patent leather shoes, white socks with lace cuffs, ruffled undershirt, a half-slip, and panties.

I just stood there, mouth agape in astonishment, at first. Then thought, why not? I'd desired fantasy. I'd come up with the first one—our rumble in the jungle. Now Dan was pulling off one of his own.

I could feel my body getting hot and tense with excitement as I put on the clothes. I had to laugh when I looked at myself in the mirror, but I liked what I saw. And I contemplated the little boy who was on the other side of the door. What type of children's games did the little pervert want to play? What would be the rules?

When he opened the door, he was dressed just as he was when I'd left him in the living room. He said nothing, only took me by the hand and led me to a large room that belonged to his friend's twin daughters.

I was caught up in a confusion of emotions. Clearly the notion of what Dan was doing was exciting me. I could feel my nipples hardening against the thin fabric of the undershirt. The crotch of my frilly pink panties was beginning to moisten.

A part of me was enchanted with the idea that Dan would make love to me in one of the canopied beds. I wanted nothing more than to take his erect cock in my mouth, to feel it probe the pink lining of my pussy.

He sat down on the edge of one of the beds and patted the coverlet. "Come here, Lizzie," he said in a paternalistic tone.

I did as I was told. He untied the pink ribbons that had held my hair in two pony tails. Then he picked up a silver-handled brush from the nightstand and began stoking my hair with it. "What beautiful hair you have. Daddy's little princess has such beautiful hair."

I was overwhelmed by a profusion of emotions—sexual, filial longings for what I had never had. Dan was all but forgotten as I was dragged under by the irresistible tide of my own needs.

"Are you Daddy's own special princess?" he asked.

"Oh, yes," I said in a kind of trance.

"And who do you love best in the whole world?"

"I love my daddy best in the whole world," I said. "There's no one in the world like my daddy." I climbing onto his lap, snuggling close to him, imagining myself young and innocent, loving a real father.

But such thoughts died aborning.

"Stand up," Dan said sternly. Then, in a softer tone, "You want to make Daddy happy, don't you?"

"Oh, yes. I'll do anything to make my daddy happy," I said, moving closer to him. Still holding the silver brush in one hand, he began rubbing the crotch of my panties with the other. Rubbing, back and forth. Back and forth.

Then he ran his hand up and down the swell of my buttocks. The silk against my skin, the friction created by the movement of his hand, was ecstasy. I could only hope that he'd hurry or Daddy's little girl was going to come where she stood.

"Daddy isn't happy with his little girl," he said, his expression darkening. "She's been naughty. She's been playing tricks and embarrassing Daddy in front of his friends. That's not a nice thing to do, is it?"

"No, Daddy," I said, looking down at my shoes.

"And what happens to little girls who make their daddy unhappy?"

"I don't know," I said, looking him in the eyes. The fantasy was taking on an edge I didn't like, but I was still caught up in it.

"Bad little girls have to be punished." He held my wrists together with one hand. His grip was firm and inescapable.

I tried to move away but couldn't.

"It's no use, Lizzie. You've been a bad little girl and now Daddy has to do something about it. He has to do something that will ensure that you never, never play tricks on Daddy again."

"Come on, Dan," I said, "this isn't funny any more."

He looked at me, his expression hard, and then hauled me over his lap, face down. He pulled down my panties. Holding me helpless with one hand, he hit me again and again with the back of the silver brush. I could hear him panting.

The blows weren't hard. They stung, though, as he kept bringing the brush down against my naked flesh, talking the whole time about what a bad girl I'd been and how I didn't deserve to be Daddy's princess. There was no actual physical pain.

But inflicting physical pain wasn't the point of all this for him. He wanted to leave a psychological mark on me. He wanted me to know that I was helpless and he was all-powerful.

On top of everything else, I was already so excited that a damp spot had formed on the side of his pants closest to my throbbing twat. I couldn't remember ever having felt so betrayed by my own body.

The spanking seemed to go on forever. When he finally stopped, he released his hold on me, but I just lay there across his knees, feeling limp, not knowing what to do. I didn't know if I was capable of getting away from him, if indeed that was what I wanted to do. I didn't know if he would let me. I had no capacity to act. And my ass stung like the devil.

I felt completely, terrifyingly passive.

"Stand up, Lizzie," Dan said at last.

I did as he ordered.

"Do you promise never to do anything like that again?"

"Yes, Daddy," I said, standing there with moisture running down my legs, the pink frilly panties now damply entangling my ankles.

"What do you have to say to Daddy?"

"I looked at floor, then quickly closed my eyes to escape the sight of those panties and my own absurd entrapment.

"I'm sorry, Daddy," I said, in a voice I could barely hear.

"I can't hear what you're saying. Look at me and stop mumbling and say it again."

I looked at him and I felt small and frightened. Some small part of my psyche obviously felt a need for his forgiveness. Looking into his cold blue eyes, I said in a louder, but still shame-filled voice, "I'm sorry, Daddy."

"That's Daddy's good little girl," he said, after a long pause. "But you look so silly standing there like that. Pull up your panties and we'll go downstairs and Daddy will give you a great big bowl of ice cream."

"But Dan," I groaned, "I feel ridiculous, and these things are a soggy mess from a very grown-up reaction to all of this. Why don't I just clean up and change back into my own clothes?"

"These are the only clothes you have," Dan lectured, refusing to drop the scenario he'd created. "Besides, little girls who wet their pants have to learn to control themselves. Now put them on, right now, before I have to spank your little bottom again. Do what Daddy says. Now!"

I did what he said, out of fear that he'd gone crazy and should be humored as much as for any other reason.

We walked down the stairs to the kitchen. He lifted me under my arms to seat me on one of the high stools that surrounded the kitchen island. Then he filled a large bowl with chocolate ripple ice cream. He scooped out a serving spoon full of it and pushed it toward me.

"Eat some of this and you'll feel much better about everything. Daddy just wants his little princess to be happy and to get everything she deserves."

Contrary to popular belief, I have a very small mouth. I could barely get it around that large spoon. Some of the ice cream spilled onto my dress. I sat there in horror, my wet panties sticking to my crotch and now gooey, chocolatey glop dripping down the front of the pink lace dress.

"You are getting to be a very messy little girl," Dan said, smiling with mockery. "We'd better get you cleaned up." He put down the bowl and spoon. "Let's go into the laundry room and put your clothes into the washer. You can't go around like that. People will think that Daddy doesn't take good care of his little girl."

We shuffled off to the laundry room. By that time I was feeling pretty stupid. Dan told me to take off all of my clothes. He watched me as I removed the dress, then said, "The chocolate has gone through to your undershirt, too. You'd better take it off and

106

wash it. And those panties and your pretty little slip need laundering. What is Daddy going to do with such a messy little girl?"

In a minute I was standing there shivering in the cold laundry room, wearing nothing but the lacy cuffed socks and the patent leather Mary Janes.

"You take everything and put it into the washing machine with the soap. That's a good girl. You've learned so quickly."

It was a front-loading machine, and I had to bend over to put the clothes in. He caressed by bottom as I did so.

"Daddy's little princess has such a sweet little behind. Daddy hopes he won't ever have to spank it again. You wouldn't want Daddy to have to do that, would you?"

"No, Daddy."

"That's my girl."

No, not his girl, I thought angrily. Not Daddy's little girl. There was no Daddy. There had never been a Daddy. There had been only emptiness. Just as there'd been, as there *was*, in my relationship with Dan Harrington. The only difference was that Dan was physically present some of the time. Now he was torturing me. Exercising a power over me that I couldn't break.

I wanted to scream, to just keep screaming until the nightmare went away.

Instead, I cried. Wasn't that just what Daddy's little girl would do?

"Lizzie, baby, don't cry. I'm sorry. Don't cry. It's all right."

I didn't know if this was the character in the strange drama Dan had created, or if he'd finally returned to normal. He made comforting noises as he picked me up and carried me upstairs to the bathroom attached to the master bedroom. It was as large as my living room, with an oversized tub sunken in the middle of an atrium setting. Everywhere, there were warm, furry rugs. Dan set me down on one of them and then filled the tub with a fragrant bubble bath.

He lifted me gently and placed me into the water. Without speaking, he bathed me, washing me first with a cloth and then with his large, now-gentle hands.

The tension eased from my body. I was relaxed, sure the bizarre fantasy had run its course, that Dan was satisfied, that he'd had his revenge. Convinced that he was once more in control, complete master of the situation, he could let it go. It was over.

He lifted me out of the tub, dried me off with a gigantic, soft towel. Then he held me in his arms. I closed my eyes, my muscles liquid from the warmth of the bath, his closeness, and the enervating effects of the water.

I wasn't aroused anymore. I wasn't angry. I wasn't frightened. I was just exhausted.

I almost fell asleep in his arms, imagining that he had set me down on the king-sized bed in the master bedroom. But when I opened my eyes, I was on one of the canopied beds in the children's room. Dan was holding up a child's flannel nightgown with comical angels on it.

"Oh, Dan, please, no more games. I'm so tired." I began to fear he'd lost his hold on reality.

"Put on your nightgown, Lizzie," he said with paternalistic authority.

I was too tired to fight, too tired to play. I didn't care where I slept, so long as I slept. I put on the nightgown.

"That's a good girl. Now Daddy will tuck you in," he said, as he put the covers around me.

I didn't know how long I'd slept when I heard a noise in the room. Dan was there, standing in the doorway, the light from the hall behind him. He was wearing only a loosely tied robe.

"I thought I heard my little girl cry out. I wanted to be sure you weren't having a nightmare. I've come to stay with you so you won't be scared."

Before I could say anything, he'd taken off the robe and was in the bed beside me. His erection was enormous. Without any preliminaries, without kissing me or talking to me, he rolled me over onto my stomach. He pushed the nightgown up. Oh, God, I thought, he's going to butt-fuck me.

I could feel the hot head of his cock probing the tight ring of my anus. I lay there completely passive and let him do it, not caring, not feeling.

When he rammed the entire length into me I screamed. I could feel every inch of him stretching and tearing my sensitive tissues. He'd done it dry, without any lubrication, the better to punish me. Each stroke was a nightmare of shooting pain until my clenched muscles finally began to relax under the assault. He quickened the pace and was soon fucking my ass as hard as he'd fucked my pussy other times. My ass felt like it was on fire as he forced his will on me harder and harder. Eventually he exploded, sending torrents of his sperm into my ass.

Oh, he reamed me thoroughly. And when he'd finished, he left the room without saying anything more.

I was asleep again in minutes.

When I awoke, I was naked on the bed in the master bedroom. My own clothes were draped across a chair. My purse and keys were on the nightstand.

There was no evidence of Dan. I got up, jumped into the shower, and then dressed. I called out to him, looked around the house for him. He was gone.

Finally, I left, almost convinced that it had all been a bad dream. The pain from the night's activities, however, was strident affirmation of its reality.

When I opened the car door, the freshly washed lace panties were spread across the driver's seat. I shoved them in the glove compartment and drove back to San Francisco.

Chapter 6

Weeks went by in which I did nothing in response to that night. Not surprisingly, I never heard from Dan. I didn't try to reach him. I felt so many different things, but most of all, I was filled with an icy cold anger and desire for revenge.

What I'd done the night of the initiation was stupid, but it wasn't intended to be malicious. Everything had simply gone too far. What Dan had done to me was premeditated cruelty. He wanted to exercise power over me, to use my deepest feelings to hurt me. It was inconceivable that he could have been so insensitive, that he felt the need to use my emotions about my father to cause such pain, to leave me feeling so violated.

His ego was more bloated than I could ever have imagined.

The night at the jungle party had been a challenge. It had been the first round of a contest, the first blow of battle. But as in all competitions, Dan Harrington had to win. He'd been the best football player, the best track star, the best businessman. Dan Harrington had been a winner all his life. Dan Harrington had been triumphant. He considered himself all-powerful.

He'd shown me that side of him that night at the house. More importantly, he'd reaffirmed it to himself.

I *could* just never see him again. I could do my best to stay away from him. My strength and self-assurance would grow if I could just avoid him long enough.

But what length of time would be long enough? How long would it be before I stopped waking in the middle of the night, my face hot with the renewed humiliation of that terrible experience? How could I let those memories be the ones that remained etched in his mind, along with the complete submission of my spirit?

As always, I threw myself into my work, hiding the turmoil inside me. But my mind, whenever it wasn't occupied by necessities, was awash with a thousand sensations that finally came together to form a magnificent revenge.

Dan Harrington would not win. Not with me.

I made all the preparations during the next week. Then I called him. I agonized over the best way to convince him to come to me. I resorted to the obvious.

I called on his private office line. I didn't get an answer the first three times I tried, which drove me wild. But I wasn't about to call on his other line and leave a message with his secretary. During the fourth attempt he answered the phone.

My voice was sweetness itself.

"Hello, Daddy," I said. "This is Lizzie. I miss my daddy. I promise to be *such* a good girl if you'll come home."

I couldn't tell if the sound I heard on the other end of the line was heavy breathing.

He didn't say anything.

"Daddy, don't you miss your little princess?"

There was more silence during which I could almost hear the gears in his brain working. Was it safe, he was wondering. Did I mean it? Ultimately his vanity would overcome his caution. Of course I'd liked what he'd done to me, he'd think. All women, no matter how independent they were on the outside, wanted to be dominated by a strong man. He would be sure of that.

"Yes," he said, at last. "Daddy misses his little princess and wants to see her."

"Can you come tonight? Please, Daddy."

It wasn't easy to sound like an innocent little girl and a woman panting for the thrust of his penis at the same time. But I managed to pull it off.

"I have to be in meetings late tonight," he said after a moment's hesitation. "But as soon as I finish, I'll come to your place. It'll probably be around one o'clock. You take a nap, like a good little girl, so that you'll be rested when Daddy gets there. Then we can play. Would you like that?"

"Oh, yes," I gushed.

"Yes, you son of a bitch," I said into the phone after I heard the dial tone.

I'd had my apartment ready for two days. I'd walked through the scenario, rehearsing as much of it as I could. Some of it would have to be readjusted according to his response. But I'd planned as much as I could, so that I could control the situation, and Dan, to my satisfaction.

Fortunately, I'd never liked having a lot of furniture and knickknacks, so my cottage was pretty spare. It didn't take much to give it an austere, spartan look. With a few appropriate embellishments, Dan had been fond of telling me, it could look like a monastery.

We all had our nightmares. I planned to bring his to life.

"Good evening, my son," I greeted him at the door.

How I savored the expression on his face. It was better than anything I could have imagined. Shock, bewilderment. That big, smug man, standing there with a giant teddy bear, grinning from ear to ear, found himself met, not by a sweet little girl, not by a seductive woman, but by a severe nun, garbed as nuns had been in less liberated times.

I loved the way his face fell. If I'd done nothing more, I would still have considered that moment my triumph.

But there was more, a great deal more.

My tone was measured, deep, authoritative but kindly…so far.

"Daniel, I'm pleased that you've brought a gift for the needy children. That's very good. But you must understand that it isn't sufficient as an act of penance. You can't buy forgiveness, not with a toy, not even when it is given with the best and purest of intentions." I wagged a finger at him. "And I don't believe your spirit is pure. But we're going to work on that, aren't we?"

He started to speak, hoping to reassert himself, to take charge, but I wouldn't let him. I kept talking, kept building the illusion. After all, the villainess of Dan's childhood, the one female power figure who had intimidated young Daniel Harrington, had been a nun. I hoped his childhood insecurities had remained with him, as mine had festered within me.

His mother, his sisters, his aunts and grandmothers, every woman, probably, he'd ever come in contact with, had adored him. But not Sister Emanuella of the Immaculate Conception School. She had despised and tormented the spoiled, beautiful boy. She had been determined to suppress the pride of the most popular boy in the school, the unmatched athlete, fantasy-darling of the young girls. She'd worked hard to break his spirit. But, Dan had always assured me, the sister had never succeeded.

I would.

I'd dressed my cottage to resemble the interior of a convent. In the entryway there was a small shrine to the Virgin Mary. The living room contained only the sofa, sans decorator pillows, and some straight-backed chairs, late of the kitchen. On the far wall I'd hung the biggest crucifix I could carry from the religious supplies shop.

I was glad that my night had arrived and would soon be over. My preoccupation with it had begun giving me nightmares of the stigmata taking over my own flesh. The idea was for the scenario to affect Dan that way.

It did. I wished I'd had a photographer handy to record his first look at the "convent." Dan hadn't set one foot inside a church since his youngest son's christening. That made it even better. There'd been no weekly doses of Sunday mass or an occasional confession to diminish the impact.

"Sit down, Daniel. It's time we had a little talk."

At first, he just stood there. He looked defiant. But the look was less a man's now than it was a strong-willed boy's.

"Sit down," I said in a voice that seemed to come from another being. I began to get into the spirit of the thing. Dan responded at once, as if in a trance. I hadn't realized it would be so easy. But I had pushed all the right buttons. The sound and the fury were enough, at least at the start.

"You are a very stubborn child. Oh, yes, I know that

115

you are well liked by the other children. But that isn't enough. You must be well liked by God. You must be the man that He wants you to be. And you know in your heart, as do I, that you have failed Him. You are not a man. You have not been what God wants you to be. Your soul is infested with sin. Your flesh, already rotted with evil intentions. The shame of what you are and what you will become is written on your face."

I could hardly keep from laughing at the somber look on Dan's face. I think he even nodded in agreement at one point.

"I must, for the sake of our Lord and for the sake of your immortal soul, do everything I can to save you from your worst self. You understand that, don't you?" I asked him. "I am doing what I must do. You must learn to obey me. You must beg our Lord for forgiveness for your sins. You must beg my pardon, for on this earth I am His representative, His bride. In the name of our Lord I must redeem your soul to regain for you the innocent goodness of the child you must once have been.

"You see, I know what you have done. The Lord knows, too, and He wants you to atone for your vile sins of the flesh."

I kept my voice steady, constant, hypnotic. It was working. I'd used one of the foolish things people tell each other in bed, in a vulnerable moment of warmth and trust. I had told Dan about my father, about my silly childhood dreams of a man who would miraculously return to me to love me and make up for all the time he'd been gone. Dan had betrayed my trust.

It was my turn.

"We know, you see, all about you and that wicked girl at Miss Meryton's. I only thank the Lord that she isn't Catholic. We can all thank the Lord that she isn't pregnant."

116

I'd triggered it all. He was flashing back.

"That's stupid," he said. "She can't be pregnant. She's still a virgin. All we did was neck. Everyone does that."

"Not everyone," I rebuked him sharply. "No good Catholic boy does. And no one, no decent person, does it in the chapel of St. Mary's Cathedral. The disgrace you have brought on yourself, on this school, on our order, can never be measured.

"You must do penance," I continued. "You must be punished. You must sanctify your flesh and beg the Lord to restore to your soul the purity that would have been yours before you violated yourself, that girl, and the church in so vile an act. You must perform an act of true contrition.

"Stand up, Daniel Harrington. Take your punishment like a man, not like the disgusting creature you have become. Let us pray together that your soul will not be damned to perdition for what you have done."

"For necking with one girl who was just as eager as I was? You must be crazy. If that girl is pregnant there's going to be a second coming, because that kid can only belong to God."

"Is there no sacrilege too great for you? You must be the most evil, wicked child who has ever attended this school. I will pray to God for your soul, which must by now surely be damned. Is there no repentance, no decency, in your heart? Can there be only monstrous sin in one so young? I must help you for the love of Jesus, our Lord. I must try to save you. Words no longer have meaning. I can see that. But for the mercy that God wants to bestow on you, I tell you to kneel down before me and pray. Pray for the sake of your eternal soul. Kneel before me now, so that you can save yourself."

"I don't kneel to a woman," Dan said peevishly

"I'll kneel to God in church, but not to some dried-up old prune who took God for a lover because no man would have her."

I slapped him across the face as hard as I could.

"Kneel, I tell you. Kneel now."

He looked at me with daggers in his eyes, just as he must have looked at her that day. I restrained myself, didn't become the hysterical bitch Dan had described to me. Instead I remained calm and in control.

"You will kneel," I said in a dead voice, "or you will regret it throughout all your days on earth and through your eternity in Hell."

"Not a chance, lady," he said, moving from me as if to leave. If I wasn't careful I would lose him, lose him as she nearly had that day. I had to establish the vestige of authority Sister Emanuella had held onto.

"You stand where you are. You do not move, or I swear to you on God's wounds that I will go to Mother Superior the instant you leave the room. She will call the bishop and your father. The disgrace to your family will brand you with infamy that will follow you everywhere. You will never be able to face your friends or anyone else. You will become in the eyes of your peers the hopeless evildoer that you are in my eyes now."

He stood still, the sound of his breathing the only clue to his frenzied state.

"You're a nasty, dirty little boy. And you will become a nasty, dirty man, filled with foul thoughts, committing rancid sins. Our Lord bled for you and His Holy Mother wept for you. And you are so hardened that it was to no avail. But I will make you see your sins, make you renounce the life you have determined to make yours. I will make you decent again."

118

Everything had gone according to plan. Dan was in my power, and I loved it. It was time to go one step further.

"If God's love cannot touch you, then I must do what I can to humiliate you and torment your flesh so that you will know what it is to suffer for the sins that man has wrought on God's earth. You stand before me in your tight jeans, your body encased in them so that you provide temptation to the innocent young women you would betray into degradation. I will show you what it is to degrade the flesh. Take them off now," I said. I lifted a ruler from the table near me.

"You must feel God's wounds. You must repent."

He obeyed. He seemed almost glad to do it. He opened the fly of his jeans. They fell to his ankles. I was prepared for what I knew I'd see—the blue silk briefs.

"Is your vanity so great, your effrontery to what is right so flagrant, that instead of decent, respectable undergarments, you wear this costume that can only have been foisted on you by the devil?" I reached into the sewing basket that I'd also set on the table and took out a pair of scissors. I came at Dan with such menacing deliberation that there was probably a moment when he wasn't exactly sure what it was I intended cutting with them. Still, he remained frozen to the spot.

I took the scissors and cut those goddamned blue silk briefs into shreds. When I was finished, they hung like ridiculous ornaments from the waistband.

He stood there, his Wilkes Bashford sweater still proclaiming who he was. But at his waist and dangling almost to his flaccid penis and balls were those tiny banners of midnight blue silk. His jeans still huddled around his ankles. The scene was ridiculous.

119

I photographed everything in my mind, determined that I'd remember every detail to my dying breath.

"You are pathetic," I told Dan. "Wouldn't it be wonderful if those boys on the track team and the football team could see their hero now? What would all those panting little girls who cheer you on to victory say if they could see you now in defeat and degradation? What would you be to them now except the repulsive, spiritual leper that you are in God's eyes and mine. But I will be kind. I will free you from your absurd entanglement. Step out from them so can you can move freely as a man, if your conscience will let you. Go into that room," I said imperiously, pointing in the direction of my bedroom. It now contained only my brass bed fitted with white sheets, a chest of drawers, a wood bench by the window, plus a crucifix over the headboard.

I ordered Dan to take hold of the brass railing at the foot of the bed. At his height it was quite a bend, just the position I'd hoped for. I took the ruler and began hitting him on the buttocks with it, my motions becoming swifter and harder. The blue tatters flew in the air currents my motions created.

I hit him again and again. I'd never had such violent intentions during my entire life as I did toward Dan that day. I was in a frenzy more thrilling than anything I had ever known as I beat him again and again, watching the welts rise in a crisscross pattern across his cheeks. I wanted to keep beating him; I wanted to make him beg me to stop.

I felt insane. Free.

There was no sound from him except deep intakes of breath in response to each stroke. He told me he'd taken Sister Emanuella's punishments like a man, no matter their severity. That was his pride, that he had come through the ordeal unbowed, undefeated.

It wouldn't be that way this day, I vowed, the rage in me inflamed by years of pain, years of letting him dominate my life while I was only a tiny corner of his.

He had everything. He had his place in the world. He had his proper little family, his wife with the right parents, his children in the right schools, his house with the right address. He had his power in the business world, his importance in the community.

He considered himself the ultimate product of the American dream.

He'd also had me. And with deliberate cruelty he had humiliated me in a scenario that he knew would tap into my deepest feelings. Then, when I was completely in his power, defenseless, he had taken me, raped my body and my soul as though I were an animal.

I hated him. I would punish him for everything he had ever done to me. The thoughts collided in my mind as I swung that ruler again and again. I couldn't even guess how long it continued. I was vaguely conscious of the sound of the ticking of the antique grandfather clock in the back bedroom. But time had ceased to have any meaning.

Finally, I stopped and ordered him to stand up and face me.

The reflection of the physical torment I'd inflicted on him was impossible to hide. He attempted unsuccessfully to mask the anguish.

I hadn't finished. I fixed my face with an expression of malevolent authority.

"Sit down, there," I ordered, pointing in the direction of the wooden bench that I'd brought in from the tiny garden behind my cottage. It was badly in need of painting and sanding.

Dan looked at me. I imagined I saw a measure of remorse, of pleading not to degrade him any further. Then he straightened himself, squared his shoulders into a posture of strength, and walked to the bench. He seated himself as proudly as he would were he placing his perfect posterior on the fifteen hundred dollar chair behind the two hundred-year-old oak desk in his office suite.

This time there was no glorious view of the bay and city surrounding him. When he sat, attempting to do so with dignity, the last of his emotional reserves, the last vestige of the man he was, gave way.

A cry of pain escaped from his mouth. Tears poured from his eyes. He made no effort to wipe them away. The first sound he'd made was the only one. He just sat there while the tears flowed.

Unfortunately, so did mine. I started to move toward him, wanting to cradle him in my arms, wanting to stop the insanity that had been released from both of us.

But, even as our tears fell, there was a look in his eyes as he perceived the softening of my expression. It was a glimmer of triumph. A wave of all-consuming hatred swept over me again. It engulfed me, drowning all other feeling, and I resumed my role.

"Look at you," I said contemptuously, "whimpering like a baby, weeping because of your twinges of discomfort. What if the Lord had wept like that before the Romans? You see yourself as a man, set yourself up as some sort of temporal god, blaspheming everything that is pure and holy in the Mother Church. And look at you. You aren't a God, only a piece of blubbering excrement. You aren't a man. A man wouldn't cry. Only filthy, cowardly little boys cry. That's what you are. How you must loathe yourself now. How I loathe you, your dirty ideas, your dirty hands that have defiled the flesh and souls of decent women. Sit there, little boy, and weep for your sins. Weep for the man you can never be."

His tears came in torrents. He was hunched over, but he still didn't raise a hand to wipe the tears away. I heard his sobs and hoped I hadn't driven him over the precipice into insanity.

Suddenly I knew the truth of it, and I was glad I hadn't retreated. Dan had altered the facts of his encounters with Sister Emanuella. Probably had fooled himself over the years. He hadn't remained defiant, ultimately in control. He hadn't left her in triumph. She'd broken him, just as I'd planned to. He had wept then. And she had gloried in it. Just as I did.

He'd been humiliated and degraded. No one but that bitter old woman and Daniel Harrington had ever known it, until now. It had all happened just days before he'd graduated from middle school, leaving the Catholic parochial system to attend a far more prestigious East Coast prep school. When he'd returned to San Francisco, he was still the legend he had always been to his family and community, destined in their eyes to vault to the top of the heap.

He'd erased from his mind the images of the pathetic child who had been beaten and broken by a woman who felt the need to degrade him, to see him finally kneel at her feet.

That had been her wicked triumph. Mine was still to be had. I still didn't have what I wanted. Lurking behind everything I'd done was the knowledge that Dan still had power over me. A welter of emotions fought for dominance over me.

Yes, I could enjoy my vicious, magnificent triumph. Mighty Dan Harrington sat before me a broken, weeping child.

I felt ashamed. There was a nurturing, kind, loving woman inside me, the woman I'd been trained to be, the kind of woman I'd read about in hundreds of novels, seen in dozens and dozens of movies and on television shows. I wanted to take the weeping boy in my arms no matter how he might respond, no matter the vestige of victory it might return to him. I wanted to give him comfort, to assure him with my kindness, my tenderness, with the gentlest part of my being that it had all been a mistake. I wanted to tell Dan that he was the man he'd always been, that every man had a bit of the child in him that made him vulnerable, lovable. It didn't diminish him in the eyes of a woman longing to give him her deepest love, her caring.

I was excited, too. I was as excited as that nun must have been beneath the protection of her holy orders. She must have been tormented by the beautiful young boy that had been Dan, his muscles already formed, his arms, thighs, strong and firm. I felt myself losing my resolve as I ran my eyes over the round, exquisite curves of his buttocks. They were gorgeous, even with the welts that covered them. His penis was large, defiant, even though the pain battled to keep it from rising to its full prominence. I could understand how that nun would have wanted him.

I wanted him now.

I went over to him, put my arms around his shoulders.

"Yes, yes, my child. Weep and God will see your tears. See that I am weeping with you, just as our Mother Mary wept for the son of God. Let our tears cleanse you of sin."

He fell into my arms, sobbing uncontrollably, a wounded child in quest of gentle consolation. I stroked his hair, then lifted his face and kissed the tears on his cheeks.

His beauty took my breath away.

When his tears stopped, I led him to the pristine white bed and sat him down. I stood before him, studying him as he looked up at me.

"God forgives you," I said quietly. "He knows that you repent. He sees your tears and loves you for them. You must be completely naked before the Lord, so that he can see you pure and cleansed of all sins."

He compliantly put up his arms as I took off his pullover sweater. I told him to stand up, which he did unquestioningly. I plucked the tattered remnants of silk from his waist, then bent quickly to remove his incongruous Gucci loafers.

What a picture we must have made—I in my full nun's habit, Dan, naked, his face stained with tears. His beautiful, once-flawless backside was striped with the wounds I had inflicted on him.

Watching his face and body, I began to remove the layers of my nun's habit. As I slowly undressed, I could see the tragic boy disappear and the man reappear in his place. I removed each portion of the religious garments, until all I had left on was my white cap. It encased my hair against my scalp so tightly that my skull ached with the tension of it.

Around my neck hung a heavy wooden rosary. I wore, as well, coarse, black cotton stockings. As I started to remove them, Dan, in his first assertive gesture, put out his hand to stop me.

For a moment I was completely in the present, waiting for him to tell me what to do, for him to take over. But the moment passed quickly.

I could see a look of rapturous adoration on his face. It was an expression I had never seen before. I realized he was in love with this ritual of pain, humiliation, and forgiveness. For the first time in all the years I'd known him, Dan Harrington was in love with me.

As that knowledge flooded over me, I reached my own climax of passion and triumph. I had an orgasm as I stood there looking at him, the heat and tremors rising in my body. His expression of admiration shone more brightly on his face. His cock was huge, veins pulsating with the intensity of his desire.

I didn't need him for anything else.

"Go away," I told him tiredly. "I don't want anything more to do with you today. I want to be by myself."

He started to come toward me. "No," I said, holding up my hand. He stopped at once. "Just go."

I didn't even look at him as he picked up his sweater and shoes, and then walked to the living room for his jeans.

My last sight of him was of his back, torn and blood encrusted with the wounds I'd inflicted.

He straightened his back and shoulders as he went through the door. His posture was unmistakably that of the Dan Harrington I'd always known.

I lay down on the bed, the skull cap pressed against my brain. I clutched the rosary. Holding it so tightly that it dug into the palm of my hand, I fell asleep.

Chapter 7

It's a frightening thing to shine a light on the darkest depths of your soul. I slept restlessly, my mind turning over what had happened the night before. I felt depraved. I despised myself, horrified at the thought of what I'd become.

Yet there was so much of it that I continued to savor. I'd never known so much power, especially over Dan Harrington. I had found the key to his psyche, although I'd used it to open my own mind to confusion and turmoil.

Mighty Dan Harrington, master of all he surveyed, admired and coveted by all women, respected and envied by men, harbored within him the need to be humiliated, punished.

I didn't care to dwell on all the reasons why. I'd let some psychiatrist do that, if the great Dan Harrington would ever allow himself to admit his dirty little secrets to a therapist. What mattered to me was that they were mine to exploit. When I gave him my love, I gave him nothing. When I showed him contempt, when I brutalized him, I provided the punishment and depravity he craved.

I knew his secret. I held power over him. I had to consider what I wanted to do with it.

No matter the twists and turns I'd experienced in my life, I had always been able to set them aside when it came to my profession. That was no longer true. I had to keep my mind free to think everything through, to consider my course of action.

I called in sick, lied that I'd had a bout of the killer flu, that I would probably be out for several days. It seemed as if I spent the better part of those days looking into the mirror. I didn't know what I was looking for in the reflection. Each time, I saw a person I didn't know. I wasn't sure I wanted to know that face in the glass.

Other people would see it, too, I thought. They'd know that I was becoming something unspeakably perverse.

I switched on my answering machine, drew all the drapes. The last call I made to the outside world that week was to the local Goodwill. I told them they could have a giant, brand-new teddy bear if they were interested in picking it up. I put it on the porch for them and then locked it and the rest of the world out.

I was going to pack away the religious props and the nun's habit, but while in the act, I knew that whatever was to come, I never wanted to be that woman again. I built a fire and threw everything into the flames. But instead of the warmth I'd hoped to feel, I experienced a sharp chill as I watched my folly turn to ashes. I imagined myself burning in the hellfire I had threatened Dan with the night before.

I'd never been very religious. I'd believed more in self-made heavens and hells on earth. And I'd delivered myself to one of those hells; I'd sold my soul to my own demons.

128

When I finished with the fire, I carried the wood
bench back to the garden. I felt a quick jab of pain
and realized that I'd gotten a splinter in my left hand.
It came out easily, but it set me to wondering if Dan
had added splinters to his newly decorated bottom.
The image touched something in the increasingly
exposed core of perversion within me and I began to
laugh. He'd looked so silly and yet so boyishly
endearing. He'd resembled a pleading child who
wanted to be dominated, punished, forgiven.

I felt excitement coursing through my veins. I
longed for him, wanted to caress his wounds.

I laughed again at the thought of him trying to
explain his stripes to his wife, or to the boys at the
gym. I imagined he wouldn't be working out for some
time. He especially wouldn't be skinny-dipping at the
Olympic Club. The giggles erupted uncontrollably.

We'd seldom talked about his wife or children. I'd
done my best to avoid thinking about them. I'd
always known that it would drive me crazy to dwell
on his domestic life. I harbored no hope that Dan
would leave her and marry me, and I had long ago
lost my desire for it. If I continued with what we'd
had it was because it would be because I wanted it.

But there was also a part of me that felt degraded
by what I had settled for—selling my emotions as
well as my body at so low a price.

Dan had said just enough, and I'd inferred just
enough to guess that all hadn't been well at his home.
He had a marriage that gave the world what it wanted to see. It wanted the illusion of perfection.

I did know that Dan never worried about how late
he returned home. Once he had let slip that he and
his wife sometimes slept in separate bedrooms. If that
wasn't the case now, I thought, he'd have to pick a
fight with her and keep it going until his butt healed.

I started to laugh again. The man who had been voted by secret sorority ballot to be the possessor of the best buns on the varsity football squad at Cal would have to keep them well hidden for a good, long time.

I anticipated being the only one who would see him before the skin healed. The thought was enticing.

I imagined Dan surreptitiously looking through the drugstore shelves in a neighborhood where he wouldn't be recognized, trying to find soothing ointments. Or would he? Just as likely, he would want to endure the pain. I could envision him flinching from the sting of it as the hot water of the shower he had surely taken as soon as he'd returned home hit his backside. I could see him standing in front of a full-length mirror, struggling behind locked doors to see the marks of his shame.

I knew ecstasy, and revulsion.

As would he. He would want more. He'd want me. I could picture him tugging on his stiffened cock until it erupted in a white torrent as he replayed over and over my treatment of him.

I would never again let him bury his fleshpole in me. I'd make him ache for me. I'd let him know what it was to want something so badly that the mere thought of it became a torture.

I wanted him to know that it was hopeless.

No, that was wrong. He had to have hope. That would make my denial even more cruel.

Late one afternoon I heard his voice on my answering machine. It was his usual casually neutral message. That way if anyone heard him and recognized his voice on my machine, it could be easily explained away as business.

"Hello," he said. "Just reporting back to you after

our last conversation. I thought the result was extremely satisfactory, with potential for increased dialogue and development. Please give me a call at my office so we can further pursue the matter."

If I'd thought about it, somewhere along the way I would have started a collection of Dan Harrington's calls, alongside a diary of the events to which those coded messages referred.

For the first time since I'd known him, I knew with absolute certainty that I would not return his call. With equally strong conviction, I knew that he would call me again.

I needed time to think.

The next morning he called me again. I let him talk to my machine. He used the same cautious coding, but I could detect something different in his voice. It wasn't quite anxiety, more a slip in the assurance that characterized his phone style.

I played the tape again and again, enjoying it more each time.

I went to work that afternoon, feeling almost normal. When I came back from my first assignment, the receptionist told me I'd received three calls from the same man, but that he hadn't left a message.

I was beginning to enjoy the strength of my position. Dan was anxious. He was worried. The calls were no longer just about his passion for more, I was sure. Now he was worried about what he had revealed, and what I might do with the knowledge.

Whatever I decided to do, I had my little Danny Boy exactly where I wanted him.

But where exactly was that? In my bed?

No, not there. I was relatively sure I'd never permit that again. It was no longer necessary to me. There were far more exciting scenarios to be explored.

The possibilities began to get me hot. I wished my

vibrator was in my desk drawer instead of on my nightstand. I needed some kind of release. I slipped one hand below the top of my desk and hiked up my skirt, my panties. I'd just inserted the finger into my pussy when one of the sportscasters who had taken me to dinner several times had the good timing to walk by my desk.

"I've got a hot tip for you," I said, still working my finger in and out of my moistening cunt. "You could score right now, if you move fast enough."

"But I've got to be on the air in twenty minutes," he whined, unaware of what I was doing. "And I haven't been to makeup yet."

"Trust me, you're going to have such a glow that you won't need any."

I withdrew my finger and jumped up. I grabbed his hand and practically dragged him out of the newsroom. Happily, at that time of day there was so much pandemonium that no one paid any attention.

I rushed him down the hall to the stockroom and pulled him inside. There was no lock on the door, but I backed up against it, pulled down my panty hose and raised my skirt. His eyes bulged from his sockets.

"Why are you just standing there? My God, no wonder the Rams dropped you. Do I have to call signals?"

He continued to look at me in utter astonishment as he fumbled with his fly. He was so nervous, I thought he was going to jam the zipper.

He was huge. And once he got over the initial shock of the moment he was fast, and good. He pulled me to him and then swiftly came up under my legs. I wrapped them around him, bracing my back against the door.

He rammed himself into me with one swift lunge, burying himself to the hilt. I begged him to fuck me hard; he was happy to oblige, his hot cock pounding deeper and deeper into me. My hips began to buck out of control against the door and my breathing was in ragged gasps.

"This feels so good," he groaned, trying to keep his voice to a whisper. When he reached his climax, he stood rigidly on his toes and buried his face in my shoulder as blasts of sperm shot like rockets out of his erect organ.

I came in a gusher just before we heard voices in the hall. I had my panty hose up and my skirt down and his zipper zipped before the knob on the door turned.

One of the secretaries walked in.

"I was sure I could find a typewriter cartridge for our hulking hero," I said to her flippantly, "but I'm not doing very well. Can you find it for me?"

She smiled mischievously as she went right to the proper shelf. They'd been in plain sight.

"Nothing like an observant reporter," I said, as she dropped a box into his outstretched hand. The secretary laughed as my stud took the box and left quickly.

I did three stories for the eleven o'clock broadcast. All of them were terrific. I left the station feeling fabulous.

I didn't even have time to check my answering machine when I came in. The phone was ringing before I could get my key out of the door. I decided to answer it.

"I have to see you," the voice said.

"Who is this?" I asked.

"Elizabeth, don't play games."

"I thought playing games was what this phone call was about."

"I want you. I want you now. I can be there in a few minutes."

"No," I said calmly. "This isn't a good time. I'm tired. It's been a long day. Besides, at 5:42 this afternoon I fucked one of the sportscasters in the stockroom at the station. And I'm just not the kind of girl who gets laid by two different men in one day."

"Bitch," he spat, and hung up.

He didn't call again for three days. When he did, his voice, no matter how hard he tried to bluff through it, was pleading. I agreed to see him.

Over the next few months we developed a number of activities that gave increasing satisfaction to both of us. But there were two things I'd vowed would not happen. I promised myself he would never actually get his cock inside of me, and that I would refrain from administering anything painful. I knew he wanted both too much.

My genital climaxes came via the jock sportscaster, who never did figure out from whence came his sudden good fortune. I even did it with him in the ladies' room one night when I was sure I was the only woman left in the building.

Then there was Dan. He came to my apartment at least three times a week. It would have been more often if I'd allowed it. I didn't know what he told his wife and I didn't care. That was his problem, and hers.

My problem was keeping up the variety of scenarios that would keep him in the secure place he wanted to be in. The common denominator was to find ways in which he was subservient, ridiculous, degraded, or downright abused. I even discovered I could combine our little games with practicality. What ensued became our Saturday afternoon ritual.

Dan would arrive, fawning, humble, calling me ma'am or Miss Renard. Then he would go straight to the kitchen, take off his clothes, and put on an apron.

Sometimes, depending on the designated tasks for the day, he'd wear rubber gloves as well.

Then he'd clean my house.

Most of the time I would ignore him, at least visibly. I'd read, listen to music, watch television. And Dan would clean away.

If I wanted something to eat or drink, I'd call him to bring it to me. "Yes, ma'am," he'd say politely. If I was feeling generous, I'd pat his bare behind as he turned back to continue his chores.

When he finished, Dan would ask me to inspect his work. If he'd done an especially good job, I would tell him so. And if I really wanted to reward him, I would let him go into my bathroom and hand wash my bras, panties, and stockings. That was the closest thing to intimacy I'd decided he was going to get from me. More than once, through the crack in the door, I saw him stop to masturbate. He would sit on the toilet or on the edge of the tub and close his eyes while stroking his cock. Sometimes he would wrap the thick, pink head in one of my bras and pump himself frantically until he came.

Some nights we'd play my own variation of Daddy's Girl. I was now immune to any psychic pain on that front. Daddy's little princess had become a prick-teasing, pubescent bitch. In my short skirts and tight sweaters, I'd go braless around the room, doing everything I could to entice him. I'd chat the whole time like a boy-crazy teenager. I'd sit on his lap describing imaginary sex scenes with boys. I'd tell him how I'd been fucked in the backseats of parked cars, under the bleachers at school, in the bedroom of a house while the boy's parents watched television downstairs. Dan never knew whether it was all fantasy or not. I think he began to believe that there were adolescent boys in my life, and the thought tormented him.

But for the sheer irony of it, I was generally on my best behavior as Daddy's girl. I would even let him touch me, and sometimes I would idly stroke his balls and penis as I told him my stories of exploratory sex. I enjoyed watching his cock swell, seeing the milky white drops that formed at its tip. I especially liked seeing his frustration at my failure to give him release.

I'd let him fondle my breasts and give me advice on how to handle boys. Sometimes I'd allow him to pretend to be in charge and let him tell me what my curfew would be and what would happen if I was late. But even in the context of the fantasy I would deny him his satisfaction. I would nuzzle his neck, or press my face against his cheek, or just brush his mouth with my lips while saying something like, "Precious, darling Daddy, don't be silly. You know you won't punish me if I come in late. Daddy is going to let his little girl do anything she wants, so that she'll keep coming home to her daddy. That way you'll be able to keep on having nice times like these."

Then I'd let him get inside my panties briefly, but only with his hands.

Sometimes when he came over I wouldn't be up to anything elaborate. And, of course, Dan wasn't permitted to initiate the action. It was all up to me. Besides, he'd never been especially creative, except for that one night in Marin.

I sometimes thought I should just administer various forms of physical abuse. But aside from the conviction that pain was what he wanted most, it was never something I felt comfortable doing. I considered all the things I could do with various kitchen utensils. But the thought never failed to sicken me. So I ignored a number of potent opportunities. I was willing, however, to essay a bit of bondage and enjoy his anticipation of what I might do.

Sometimes I strove for elegant simplicity. Once I tied his hands so that he was slightly bent over the footboard of my brass bed. Then let him watch me masturbate as a I lay just beyond his reach. I ran my fingertips along the edge of my pussy, then let him see me slowly part the lips. I was unbelievably wet; my fingers slid in easily. I loved bringing those fingers to my lips and licking them off as Dan watched helplessly. Then I plunged them back in and almost abuscd mysclf for the pleasure of seeing him writhe.

I would enjoy flicking my tongue across his lips, or setting my lips on his. I'd open them wide enough for a French kiss and then pull away. I developed a few variations on that theme, nothing elaborate, maybe a slight alteration in my fleeting contact with him, or a change of costume. Mostly I'd wear standard stuff— a black garter belt and stockings and other Frederick's of Hollywood-style paraphernalia. I was rarely totally nude. It seemed banal somehow after all we'd done.

Another night I greeted him in a sheer, virginal, white negligee and peignoir. As I might have done anytime back in the old days, I kissed him and let him kiss and fondle me. Then I led him into my bedroom. I'd put soft music on the stereo, and I was drenched in his favorite perfume. Champagne was chilling on the night stand.

I helped him to take his clothes off, folding them carefully and putting them inside the chest at the foot of the bed, except for his silk tie. I instructed him to sit and relax on the bed. Then, continuing to speak softly, seductively, I came up behind him, drew his hands together, and bound them with his tie.

I slid around in front of him and tied his ankles

together with a scarf he'd given me for Christmas one year. I'm sure his secretary had picked out that scarf, thinking it was for Dan's wife.

"I want to explain something to you, Dan," I said, my tones dulcet, my voice soothing, my hands caressing his body. I touched his chest, legs, inner thighs, but never quite the spot where he wanted to be touched the most. "In a minute I'm going to put you in my closet. You won't be uncomfortable in there. It's large enough for you. You can stand, sit, or lie down, whichever you prefer. There's no lock on the door and I've decided not to gag you, so you'll have to be on the honor system and be still and silent.

"A friend of mine is coming for a visit. If you make any sound or movement that tips him off that you're here, I'm going to open the doors and let him see exactly who is in the closet. Do we understand each other?"

He nodded.

"And you're going to behave?"

He nodded again.

"That's good. Now it's almost time, so you'd better get in there." He was just the proverbial hop, skip and a jump away from the closet. He shuffled there quickly and settled himself. He didn't look particularly comfortable; no closet was intended to conceal a man his size.

We'd finished just in time. The doorbell rang. "Not a sound. Remember," I said as I closed the door. I went to greet my sportscaster in the same manner I had originally used with Dan.

But, of course, the direction of our activity was quite different. My bed became our playing field. Cerebrally he wasn't much, but that wasn't what I wanted from him. And while there was little art to his technique, he had an athlete's agility.

138

I could feel Dan's eyes boring into me as I rasped, "Stick that big fuck-pole into me. Split me wide open. I want my cunt full of your cock." Then, virtually right in front of him, my jock ran his cock along my lips before plunging deeply into my cunt. His balls dragged along my pubis with each stroke. I could hear their slap, slap as he drilled me. I knew Dan could hear it, too. That was just what I wanted.

"Shoot me so full of your come I can taste it in the back of my throat," I screamed, grinding my hips.

He gave a native South Carolinian's rebel yell when he came. It was a charming touch, I thought.

I responded in kind, reacting far more vocally than was my norm in such situations.

I wanted them both to have a good show.

A few more glasses of champagne, one more go-round and my sportscaster was exhausted. He fell into a deep, snoring sleep. I slipped out of bed and into the closet, untied Dan, shoved his clothes at him, and told him to get out.

He stopped long enough to cast a look of sheer hatred at the slumbering man in my bed.

In my efforts to find new amusements, I considered the leather, boots, whip, dominatrix scene. But it seemed so typical under the circumstances. Besides, I couldn't take the chance of being recognized in one of those sleazy Folsom Street shops where they sold the appropriate accouterments.

Most importantly, my vanity demanded creativity. I'd always taken great pride in my work and my play.

I didn't quite know what I was unleashing when I came up with a new twist for my Saturday encounters with Dan.

There was pain involved, but not of the traditional S&M variety. I wouldn't be satisfied with that for Dan Harrington. I planned to introduce him to the conventional physical tortures that women, especially women of previous generations, had accepted as simply routine.

It wasn't easy assembling a full ensemble for someone six foot three inches tall with a corresponding build and shoe size. But it was worth the effort when I examined all I'd found—from pointed toe pumps to blond wig.

The undergarments were my particular pleasure. I delighted in the contemplation of Dan Harrington encased in every sartorial torture known to preliberated modern woman.

I had it ready for him when he arrived that Saturday. Cleaning day would wait. I had other plans.

I gave him time to undress in the kitchen, but before he could put on his apron, I told him to come to the bathroom. I instructed him to sit on the edge of the tub. Then I soaped up his legs and underarms and took out my razor.

His hair wasn't very visible, so light a blond was it. But I wanted my vision to be perfect.

He started to object when I shaved his legs, then thought better of it. I didn't believe he'd be in any danger of discovery at the gym or that his wife would get close enough to him to see his hairless hide. So I proceeded with my plan and shaved all the hair from under his arms. To complete his toilette, I even tweezed a few errant hairs from his eyebrows.

It was such fun.

I covered him with my body lotion in his favorite fragrance, topping it off with cologne and dusting powder.

I made up his eyes, heightened his cheekbones, and gave him a full, red mouth. For all his size and masculinity, Dan made a not unattractive woman. I stood back and admired my work. But I didn't let him

140

look. Not yet. I placed the wig on him, anchoring it to his thick hair with hair pins. He looked great—from the neck up.

I was feeling kindly, so I didn't paint the nails on his fingers and toes. Besides, I'd already concluded that both needed to be covered. Standing him in front of the nineteenth century cheval mirror in my bedroom, I handed him a full girdle, complete with garters and a pair of ladies hip-hugger panties, both of which I'd guessed would be one size too small.

"You put the panties on first," I told him. He watched himself in the mirror as he stepped into them and pulled them up. I could see his displeasure as the material accentuated areas that had gone to flab. Time Dan would normally have spent in the gym working them off had been spent with me.

"Don't worry," I said encouragingly, "the girdle will take care of all that." It was quite a sight watching Dan pull and tug that iron monster up over his thighs and hips, finally twisting it into place. The stockings were next, stretched and pulled until he'd attached them to the back garters.

Next, I handed him a waist-cinching, boned, long-line bra. I'd stuffed the breasts with rubber pads, and adjusted the straps so that they dug just slightly into his shoulders. Finally, I gave him three-inch, spiked pumps and told him to practice walking in them.

He actually did rather well, but I told him to keep at it so that I could savor the image of him mincing around in that hideous girdle and bra. They dug into him terribly, and I delighted at the thought of the marks they'd leave on his skin when he took them all off.

I sat down in the chair next to my dressing table. "Come here, Daniella," I commanded. "I want to admire you up close, you magnificent creature."

I was disappointed to see he was having a great time. He swayed his hips, sashaying up to me flirtatiously.

"You know, you're a real looker," I said, as he stood in front of me. "Yup, a real dish," I muttered, while I ran my hand up the inside of his legs. Damned if he didn't giggle. "Now let's see the rest of the ensemble."

I made him put on a not-very-exciting, utilitarian slip and a polyester print dress. It was all rather dowdy, which had been what I'd intended, but upon seeing the result I decided to get more fashionable the next time around.

"Let's go into the living room," I said cordially. I sat on the sofa, Dan on a straight-backed chair that I was sure put pressure on his garters. I served him a plateful of little tea sandwiches and poured him cup after cup of Twinings' special blend.

I knew that, before long, it would all have to pour out again.

At first he tried to sit like a man, legs comfortably apart, but quickly realized that in the long, tight girdle, that just wasn't comfortable. Then he tried sitting with his legs together, crossed at the ankles. He looked wonderfully prim and silly.

Finally, he crossed his legs, adjusting the hem of the dress so that it would creep up and expose the bottom of the girdle and the tops of his stockings. I was grateful I'd been one generation too late for all that discomfort, and I wondered that the stuff could even still be found in stores. What kind of woman still went in for that kind of masochism?

Despite everything, Dan and I carried on a pleasant, matter-of-fact conversation, something we hadn't done in weeks. He talked in a normal voice about things that were happening in the office and the

142

Business League. I talked about stories I was working on.

Eventually, he began to squirm. His discomfort, and his uncertainty about what to do, became evident.

"Do you need to use the powder room?" I asked, simpering ever so slightly. "If so, you're excused."

"Yes, thank you," he said with relief. It was quite some time before he returned.

"I thought I'd never get out of all of that," he admitted. "I couldn't figure out what to do first—hold up the skirt, pull down the girdle and pants, or undo the stockings and try to take off the pants without taking the girdle off."

"You should try it after waiting ten minutes in line during the first intermission at the Opera House," I said.

"I couldn't."

"Yes, you could. Maybe we should do just that sometime." I laughed. "Now don't look so worried. It was just a joke. I think it's much better if we keep this to ourselves. Another sandwich?" I asked politely.

Weeknights were still open to experimentation and variety. But Saturdays evolved into a relatively set pattern of events.

When Dan arrived, generally in the late morning, I would permit him to go straight to the bedroom. His ensemble would be prepared for him. The rest of the day would follow according to the outfit I'd chosen.

If it was a utilitarian maid's uniform, along with practical cotton underwear, sturdy shoes, and support panty hose, it meant it was a cleaning day. If there was a cute little French maid's uniform, all frills and décolletage, it meant he was to go into the bathroom, shave his legs and underarms, and make up his face.

143

He'd gotten quite good at it. His underwear on those occasions consisted of a lacy black bra, sheer, crotchless panties, black lace stockings, and a garter belt. The look was completed with fuck-me, high-heeled sandals. Work included lots of bending over and flirtation on his part.

If it was a traditional outfit, it meant I still expected him to shave and put on makeup, but wanted him to modify it to fit the style. I always selected the jewelry to complete the look, but I began to think Dan could have done it.

With each outfit, there was always some form of girdle. I chose tight-fitting, constricting costumes so that girdles were a necessity. I sometimes thought that Dan deliberately let himself gain a few extra pounds just for the thrill of enduring the discomfort. If I'd been able to, I would have given him premenstrual cramps as well. But then the ecstasy might have been too much for him.

When the lady's ensemble was ready for him, it usually meant that I had already made lunch and that he would be my guest. We would while away the afternoon chatting until it was time for him to change his clothes and go home. I never said so, but the impression I wanted to create was that he had to leave because I had a date in the evening. Generally, this wasn't untrue.

The sportscaster and I had become quite an item. In addition to our trysts, we'd been seen about town enough to fuel speculation in both Herb Caen's and Rob Morse's columns that we might be headed for a wedding. I sometimes worried that the sportscaster was getting the same idea. I would carefully steer clear of the subject whenever it appeared in conversation.

The following Saturday when Dan arrived, I

directed him to a lady's costume I'd set out for him. I was dressed similarly. This time, though, there was also a brimmed hat and gloves. That way he'd be able to cover his enormous hands. I laughed when I saw him. He looked like a transvestite, but it wasn't impossible that he could be a very large woman.

I handed him a purse and a pair of sunglasses and said, "It's time to take this show on the road. We're going out to lunch."

"Oh, no we're not," he insisted. But he only went through the motions of protest. He was actually as intrigued by the idea as I was.

I drove us to a restaurant on Sacramento Street that had a patio area as well as a dining room. It was late spring and unseasonably warm for San Francisco, but the fog was still on the bay, ready to cool everything off. It was a stretch, but a woman might want to keep her gloves on while eating alfresco.

Dan drew a certain amount of attention. But, after all, we *were* in San Francisco. Whatever his sexual orientation, he was dressed tastefully, fashionably. And we behaved well. No one bothered us. I had my hair tucked up under my hat and, like Dan, kept my sunglasses on. I doubted anyone would recognize me.

It went well. Dan wasn't very good at speaking in a falsetto voice, but since it was unlikely a woman his size would have one, he didn't even try. We both kept our voices low. Fortunately, no one was seated at the table next to us.

We were enjoying coffee when Dan's face suddenly blanched and he gasped, "Oh, God!"

"What is it?"

"The woman who just sat down at the table in the corner...that's my wife!" he choked.

I couldn't help but laugh.

"This isn't funny," he growled, *sotto voce*.

"Are you kidding? It's hysterical." But I did try to control myself. I didn't fancy a public scene any more than he did, although it would have been the ultimate revenge.

"Have you ever dressed up in women's clothes in front of her?" I asked in a subdued tone.

"Are you crazy? Of course not."

"Then relax. It's not exactly something she'd expect. She's not going to recognize you. Stay calm. I'll get the check and we'll get out of here before she has a chance to get a good look at you."

I couldn't help but look her over with a reporter's eye. She was blonde—washed-out, old-money blonde. She looked like the kind who was born to join the Junior League, who wore sensible, but very expensive, low-heeled shoes. She was the type who'd blend in perfectly with the upper middle-class masses at Trader Vic's or the Burlingame Country Club.

For just a second I wanted her to see the face of my lovely companion. It would have been such fun. But if there'd been a scandal, my career and reputation would have been ruined along with his. And though I was willing to go on playing with fire for the rewards it brought to my ever-expanding psyche, I wasn't ready to throw myself directly onto a funeral pyre.

Surprisingly, it was Dan who couldn't resist the challenge. There were two ways we could have left the restaurant. By taking one, we would have been at a safe distance. The other took us right past her table.

Before I could steer him to the safer route, he was off in her direction. I could do nothing but follow. As we passed her table, he said in a high voice, with just the right degree of Long Island lockjaw, "Don't you just love that scarf?"

146

Once we were safely ensconced in the car, we both collapsed into laughter.

Such brazen courage deserved a reward. So the next Saturday, I had him don the French maid's uniform. While he dressed, I retired to the guest room, took off my clothes, and put on a flaming red, ultra-sheer baby-doll nightgown. I returned to my bedroom just as he was finishing his toilette.

"Danielle," I said as I posed in the doorway, "I think we should make love."

I helped him to remove everything except his lace panties, satin garter belt, and fishnet stockings. We would, I had decided, make love as two women. He understood that without receiving instructions from me.

We kissed deeply, stabbing each other with our tongues. He caressed and nibbled at my breasts, marvelling at the way my nipples swelled to meet his lips. He circled my twat with his tongue, then took my clitoris between his teeth. He sucked and licked it gently, bringing me to a near orgasm. I ignored the bulge in front of his panties, but fondled him everywhere else.

Finally, I reached to the nightstand for my dildo and handed it to him.

He didn't waste time. He buried it in the folds of my cunt almost viciously, licking along the outer edges as he manipulated it with expert fingers. His breath came as raggedly as my own as he maintained the in-out, in-out motion. He increased the pace when he saw how wet I became and fondled my clit at the same time. It was heavenly and relaxing. It didn't take too long for my juices to start running down over his fingers. Then he switched hands, bringing the moist fingers to his mouth.

We fell asleep close to each other. It was all rather sweet.

One might wonder why I never dressed as a man or otherwise played the masculine role. But it was something I never wanted, was never even momentarily tempted to do. I could have gotten terribly analytical about it, but I believed my reasons to be pretty basic and simple. I just didn't have any desire to be a man or to assume masculine traits, anymore than I'd set out to make Dan behave like a woman. It just happened that one of a variety of scenarios I'd prepared had worked out especially well.

In fact, except for the incident in the restaurant, it had all begun to bore me. I needed something new, always something new.

That fact, that need, was beginning to prey on my mind.

Chapter 8

I felt a definite need to expand my sphere of influence. It was one thing to have Dan within my power once he'd entered my portals, but I wanted to know I had him all the time. I kept thinking about our little foray to the restaurant. I wanted more.

I also recognized that I needed to come up with new and interesting games to keep him interested. If I wavered or ceased to find new excitement and perversions, I knew I could wind up as just one more diversion, and not the most important one, in his life. Now that I'd done all the work and opened the door to his psyche, he might even have gone on to find someone else willing to explore its labyrinthine corridors with him.

I'd begun to get insecure despite the knowledge that he'd have been insane to let anyone else in on his sick little secret. But then, we were both slightly insane. I knew it with absolute clarity of vision.

In some ways, nothing had changed from the old days. All of the burden was still on me to make something happen. On the other hand, I was having a lot more fun...at least some of the time.

The next Saturday when he arrived for "just us girls" day, I set out only the basic white girdle, cotton bra, and neutral-colored support stockings for him. Dan in costume and character as a woman was one thing. But I wanted to see what would happen to Big Dan Harrington if no persona had been provided for him.

When he went in my bedroom to undress, I called out to him, "Don't put on the wig or any make-up. I have other plans for you."

Then I went into the kitchen, microwaved some popcorn, took a six-pack of Anchor Steam beer from the fridge, and carried everything into the living room. I turned on the 49er's game.

"What dress do you want me to put on?" he called out cheerily.

"None," I said. "Come on out."

Yes, it was just what I'd hoped for. Fully clothed and made up, he could almost pass as a human being. There was an element that made it acceptable, like someone dressing up for a costume party.

Without that element he was just a big man—awkward, uncomfortable—who looked ludicrous in hideous women's underwear. He took in the room at a glance, what it was set up for, and eyed me warily.

"It's been a busy, tough week for both of us," I said casually. "I thought it would be nice to just sit around and relax. You like football, and I know you miss the Saturday games when you're here with me. I wanted to make it up to you. Just sit down and have a beer." I smiled sweetly.

"Like this?" he asked, gesturing at himself.

"Yes, of course. Why not? You've never objected to anything I've picked out for you to wear before."

It was just as I thought. He hadn't minded playing a character. I'd taken that away from him, dissolved

150

the barrier between the two sides of Dan Harrington.

He could refuse to obey and leave. But that would have changed the rules of the game.

If he objected, he gave me victory. Even now, by his inability to hide his discomfort, he was giving me a small win. I wanted to hold onto it, to keep him from finding a way to make my slap in the face acceptable to him. But of course, I knew he would do just that.

"You're right," he said at last, "there's no reason this shouldn't be just as interesting and maybe even as stimulating as everything else we've tried."

"It's certainly working for me," I said, stuffing my face with a handful of popcorn.

Dan tried to look self-possessed watching the game, drinking beer, cheering the home team. The beer was a killer, much worse than the tea.

"You're not very good at this," I laughed, as he nearly lost the battle with his girdle in the bathroom. "You need more practice." I could see that he was finally out of it. He raised the toilet seat and started to aim. "No, not that way," I said. "Do it like a lady." For a second I thought he might aim it right at me. But then, very quickly, he did as he was told.

Yes, Dan as Dan in a girdle was really something special.

He didn't drink much the rest of the game. As soon as it was over, he announced that he was going and went into the bedroom to put on his own clothes. I followed him.

"No, don't do that," I said as he started to unhook the bra. This time it lay flat and sort of wrinkled against his chest. It hadn't seemed appropriate to fill the cups.

"I told you I'm going."

"I know. But I want you to keep it on."

"You're crazy."

"Obviously. But that doesn't alter the fact that I want you to keep it on."

"I can't go out like this."

"I don't expect you to. You can put your clothes on over what you're wearing."

"No."

"Fine. Don't come back."

"Why this?"

"Because I like it," I said petulantly. "If you wear it, it will make me feel that what we have together will be with you wherever you are."

"All right," he growled, "if it will make you happy, I'll wear them out of here. I'll ditch them later."

"Oh no. I want you to wear them all the time. I want you to wear them under your suits at the office, under your casual clothes, under your sweats when you jog. You need to jog, you know. You're getting flabby. And you won't want to go to the gym. It would be awkward getting undressed. And then there'd be those garter and girdle marks and all. Besides," I said, giving him a promise of things to come, "you never know when there might be something new to keep under wraps.

"Wear them, Dan. Wear them all the time. I have to know that you're wearing them," I said breathlessly, absently stroking my breasts.

"What am I going to do with them when they're off?"

"You have separate bedrooms and bathrooms now. Just take them off at night and wash everything. You've had practice with that."

I wasn't supposed to see him until Wednesday night. Late Tuesday morning, before I left for work, I called him. When he answered, I asked, "Are you wearing them?"

"Yes," he said.

"I hope you're not lying to me. I could come down there and check, you know. In fact, that's just what I'd like to do, come right now, take down your pants, and reach up in that tight casing and squeeze your balls. You'd like that, wouldn't you?"

"Yes," he said in a hoarse voice. Then he added in a more normal tone, "That's all for now, Miss Winslow. I'll talk to you about those letters later this afternoon."

"Wouldn't your secretary like to know what's under your shirt and pants?" I said. "Dan, is she gone?"

"Yes."

"Then get up and lock the door."

"Why?"

"Just do it." The phone rattled as he put it down. He returned a moment later.

"Now I want you to do something just for me and for yourself. Are you sitting in that big, wonderful chair of yours?"

"Yes."

"Good. Now unzip your pants and let them fall to the floor. Are you doing that?"

"Yes," he responded hypnotically.

"Okay, now I want you to reach under the girdle up to the crotch of the panties. And then I want you to imagine that it's my hand there and do what you'd want me to do. Go ahead Dan. I'm just sitting here on my bed, my legs spread in a special new pair of stirrups I bought just for you.

"And I'm using my vibrator where it will do the most good. Can you hear it? When I come, I want to know that you're coming too. Just keep rubbing Dan. Feel the friction. Feel me." I could picture his fist wrapped around his cock, pumping, stroking.

153

He let out a sharp cry, the variety I remembered from less complicated days in the bedroom. And I knew that I'd accomplished my purpose. I went on painting my toenails.

"Was it good for you, Dan?"

"Yes," he said nearly inaudibly.

"Good, now aren't you glad you did as you were told?"

"Yes."

"I'll see you tomorrow night, then."

The stirrups were suspended by straps from a hook originally used for a potted plant. They were attached to the ceiling just beyond the foot of my bed. When Dan arrived the next night, I stopped him just inside the door to put my hand in the top of his pants and check for the girdle. Then I told him to go into the bedroom, get undressed, and lie down on the bed. I wasn't in the mood to watch him struggle out of the girdle. Besides, he'd been getting better at it and it had started becoming less fun to watch.

He was stretched out naked on the bed when I came in. His cock was standing at attention.

"How do you like the new addition?" I asked.

"Interesting," he said calmly, but I could see that he was practically salivating in anticipation.

"It's going to get even more interesting," I said, putting a pair of leather cuffs around his wrists and then attaching them to the chains that I then connected to the headboard. I lifted his feet into the stirrups.

Dan was in a glory of discomfort and excitement. I expected him to ejaculate any second from the thrill of it all.

Actually, I didn't have much planned for that night. I mostly wanted to get Dan used to the idea of being chained until I saw fit to release him. Oh, I did a whole lot of obvious things, like tickling him with ostrich feathers and putting ice cubes on his balls. I even put a candle just a teeny way up between his buttocks, not nearly as far as I think he would have liked it. Which is why I stopped.

Then I held the blade of a knife against his penis. "Does this make you nervous?" I asked.

"No," he said, "I trust you."

"Why thank you, Dan. That's sweet."

He had every reason to go right on trusting me through most of the initial bondage stage. Frankly, I'd become so preoccupied at work that, between keeping up with his underwear collection and keeping him moderately amused when he came over, I had little time and energy for anything else.

Some of the time, I worried again about him not coming back if I failed to maintain my creativity. But I'd been getting more confident about the whole thing and I didn't want to spoil him.

Events slipped into a kind of pattern. I had begun working on some special assignments most Saturdays, so that eliminated our liaisons. When he came over during the week he'd get naked and I'd strap him into a harness that was attached to chains hooked on the curtain rod in the hall doorway. He'd content himself with wandering around the house like some sort of pornographic version of Marley's ghost while I worked.

I did get more expansive in my selection of underwear for him. I would have been even more so—I had my eye on some really nifty teddies and dance pants—but Dan had gotten so deeply into bondage that anything less constricting than fifties-style girdles would have disappointed him. I did try to find the prettiest ones I could for him in a rainbow assortment of colors with matching bras and color-coordinated stockings. I wanted him to feel pretty inside.

That should have kept him happy, but it wasn't nearly enough. One night when he became especially annoying I gave him a smack on the butt with my Lucite clip board. It made him even more frisky and demanding.

I really didn't want to hit him, but he wanted it so badly.

I went to the kitchen and found a copper pot I'd recently bought. I brought it back into the living room and said, "If I give you a few good smacks with this, will you settle down and watch television or something and let me get my work done?"

He agreed instantly. I whacked him about six times on the butt. His skin turned bright red. I hoped that would be sufficient. He quieted down and I went back to work.

I pretty much forgot about him for the next hour or so. Then I happened to glance toward the bedroom. Dan was sitting on the floor masturbating while he watched Joan Rivers.

That man was really into pain.

Chapter 9

There were things I thought I could never, ever do. At one time it probably included most of what I'd been doing the last several months. But I liked to believe that even I had limits.

Then, one morning, I opened the paper and saw the news in the social column. Dan Harrington and his wife were splitting up. It was a "blind item," but there was enough information in the cutesy, teasing little paragraph that there was no mistaking who it was about.

The bastard had never even hinted that it might happen.

I was in a rage.

I had the day off and Dan was coming over that night. All day I fumed, wishing that he didn't enjoy pain so much, want it so much, because God knew I wanted to give it to him. And I didn't want him to derive one moment of pleasure from it.

By the time he arrived I was so angry and frustrated and in such a state that I could have done just about anything. When I went to court on murder charges I'd have stood there and calmly defended my actions in the absolute belief that everything I'd done was completely justified.

Dan was in a jaunty state of mind, feeling full of himself about some big deal he'd just closed. He actually expected enthusiasm and praise from me. I could only conclude that he'd forgotten who I was and what we were doing. He must also have forgotten that I could read.

I smiled enthusiastically and said, "Your success calls for a special celebration."

I took him by the hand and led him into the bedroom. As if everything was going to proceed normally, I helped him to undress, caressing his chest as I undid his shirt buttons.

"You're certainly in a kittenish mood," he said, so pleased with life and himself.

Dan liked to think that I was still so much in love with him that I would gladly have spent the rest of my life in bed with him if that was the way he wanted it. He was delighted with the idea that he could bring out the old, adoring Lizzie and enjoy the pleasures of her.

I'd kept the notion alive, enjoying coming so close and then pulling away.

When he was completely undressed, I told him to lie down on his stomach. I was sure he thought I was going to give him a full body massage.

"Just relax, darling," I said, reaching for his tie. I took hold of his hands and encircled them, then bound them the headboard with several knots.

I'd never realized when I'd bought the bed the range of services it would provide.

I used the suit pants of his suit to tie his legs. He wasn't pleased with the use I was making of his wardrobe.

"Is there anything you want to tell me, Daniel?"

"I already told you my news."

"Are you sure that's all?" I urged him. He didn't notice the dangerous look in my eyes.

"All that's important."

"Really, what an interesting set of priorities you have. See this," I said as I held up a wire hanger. "Well, Mommie Dearest isn't the only one who knows how to use it. And I'm not planning to hang up your jacket with it." I ran the edge of it along his spinal cord.

"Are you sure there isn't anything else you want to tell me?"

It was really stupid of me to threaten. He just thought it was a game. I could see the thrill of anxiety rush through him.

He didn't want to miss a shot at the first really good beating he'd had in ages.

Oh, I didn't want to do it. He still had scars from the past beatings. And yet it was still so beautiful, that ass of his, even with a few extra pounds and the marks left by the girdle on it.

I wanted to caress it, not shred its flesh.

But then I remembered that newspaper paragraph and I saw red, and that's how I wanted to see his butt. I raised the coat hanger and brought it down again and again.

"Talk to me, Dan," I choked out. "Tell me what I want to know."

I was in a frenzy, only vaguely aware that I had passed his pain threshold. Then I regained a vestige of sanity and awareness.

He was gasping with pain. I knew he was desperate to cry out for me to stop.

But, of course, he couldn't.

"Tell me about it Dan. Tell me what half of San Francisco knows and you haven't bothered to tell me."

"All right, all right" he sobbed.

Thank God, I thought, and threw down my weapon. His whole backside was a bloody pulp. I was frightened and shaking, but I couldn't let Dan see that.

"Just let me get my breath," he said in short, hoarse spurts. The pain must have been excruciating. There was no longer any hope of hiding my horror at what I had done.

"No, don't say anything. Don't try to talk. Oh, God, I'm sorry. I'm so sorry. I must be going insane. How could I have done this?" My hand hovered over his skin, afraid to touch it.

"Maybe we should call a doctor."

"Don't be foolish," he said. "We can't do that. Just wash it clean. Do you have any peroxide?"

"Yes," I answered meekly and went to the bathroom to get it.

Dan was calm, commanding, in control. The pain had obviously subsided.

When I put the peroxide on his wounds the sounds he made were of sick pleasure. My concern, my contrition, had been nothing to him but an admission of weakness.

I wanted to untie him, help him into his clothes and get him out of there. I wanted to tell him to get out of my life before either of us became any more demented.

But his voice—that cool, calm, superior voice—tormented me.

I would continue. I was entangled in it. I was turning into a sadistic barbarian.

"Tell me about your wife," I said in a flat tone as I continued my mop-up operations on his back.

In an equally unemotional voice, he said, "She left me three weeks ago."

"I see. And when were you planning to tell me?"

"I don't know. There were things I had to think about, the changes it would make in our equation."

"And have you come to any conclusions?"

"Not yet."

"I see. Well, then, would you mind telling me exactly how this astonishing event came about?" I asked as I untied him. "No, don't sit on my sheets, you'll ruin them. The blood hasn't clotted yet. Get dressed. But keep talking."

He winced as he put on the corset I'd bought for him as a special treat. It was a French import trimmed with lace and ribbons.

"I was really exhausted one night after back-to-back meetings from breakfast through dinner," he related, as he continued to dress. He sat gingerly on the edge of the bed. "When I got home, I got undressed and fell into bed. I left my clothes in a heap on the floor, including that black girdle, garter belt, and stockings. My wife came in the next morning to talk to me about something relating to the kids. I was still in bed. Out of habit, she picked up my clothes."

"Good lord," I interjected, "she realized she was married to a transvestite."

"No, of course not," he scoffed. "That would never occur to her. She was sure that I was having an affair, and that they were some kind of trophy. She was incensed with the possibility that I might even have had the woman in the house."

"Didn't she notice the size? Did she think you were fucking an Amazon?"

"She didn't stop to measure them. She just dropped them, told me to fuck myself, and ran screaming from the room. When she calmed down, she called her lawyer. They served me with the papers the next day and I moved out that night."

161

"Where?"

"To an apartment."

"Where?"

"On Nob Hill, not far from the place I had when I first met you."

"So, your wife thinks you're having a nice, ordinary affair with another woman and she threw you out. Can you imagine what she'd do if she knew the truth?"

"She does know part of the truth."

"What are you talking about?"

"I *am* having a nice, ordinary affair, with a very nice, very young woman. I see her every night when I'm not here. I need you, Elizabeth. I need what we have here. But I also need balance, normalcy, womanly affection, normal sex."

Daniel Harrington is living proof that I am incapable of murder. All I could think of to say was, "Get out of here, now."

"Yes, that's a good idea. We'll talk about it in a couple of days, when you're calmer."

"You patronizing son of a bitch. We won't talk about anything. Don't call me. Don't ever come here again."

"Why do you waste time saying things like that when you must know that even if you mean them now, you won't mean them three minutes after I'm out the door. Let's not waste our time, Elizabeth."

I had achieved nothing. I'd fooled myself once again.

"Swear to me that you'll never see her again."

"I'm not going to do that."

"If you ever want to come here again, get down on your hands and knees and beg my forgiveness. And swear that you'll never see her again."

"You know that I'm not going to do that. Why do

you aggravate yourself? Your trouble is that you always want more than it's possible to have."

He was the same old smiling Dan Harrington, even with his backside a pulpy, stinging mess.

I vowed that one day I would bring him to his knees.

"Do you want to punish me for being unfaithful to you? What do you imagine that you can do to me that I won't enjoy?

"Now try to be reasonable, Lizzie. We both have what we need. You have your jock from the station. I have my nice, pretty young woman. This isn't the only thing I want. I need a release. I may be a pervert, but I'm only human."

"Well, you go to your sweet little woman. And try to explain the welts on your butt."

"I won't have to. I'll just tell her that for tonight I'd prefer to make love in the dark. She won't ask any questions. She'll just accept it. She wants to make me happy.

"She'll do whatever I want. Just as you do, Lizzie. Just as you do."

I could think of nothing to say as he hobbled out the door.

Chapter 10

The power had remained his. No matter what I'd done. He'd won. I'd beaten him until he bled. I'd felt animalistic, barbaric, sick. Dan Harrington had loved it. To him it was more than the joys of pain and humiliation. It was one more macho triumph. Dan Harrington liked to prove he could endure anything and still be Dan Harrington.

I tried to convince myself that I had to stop, that I had lost, that I would keep on losing. Yet, I had to go on. There had to be a victory for me in the end.

He didn't call.

Twelve days after our last meeting I called him and invited him over for a special treat—something that had just arrived from Stockholm in a plain brown wrapper. I was surprised when he agreed to come.

As soon as he'd arrived I told him to take off his clothes. That much was normal. When he was naked, I strapped him into a black leather harness that wrapped around the top of his legs to his waist, much like a pair of briefs, except that it had a large, round section cut out at the back and a smaller aperture in the front so that the balls and penis were free of confinement. It wasn't intended to cause any discomfort. No doubt that was an immediate disappointment to Dan.

It closed at the sides with a strap and lock. It also had a small loop and detachable chain, which I used to connect it to the bed. The contraption had just enough slack so that Dan could sit up and watch the bedroom television.

I ran a video I'd made. It wasn't terribly well done, but hiding a camera among the clothes in my slightly open closet hadn't been easy. It was about thirty minutes in length and contained some of my favorite moments with five different men on that very bed. Over the natural moans and groans on the tape, I also did a live commentary.

His face and balls turned bright red, but he managed to stay verbally noncommittal.

When the show was over, I removed the chain and told Dan to go home. He told me to unlock the harness.

"No, I think you should keep it on for a few days. Then you can come back and I'll take it off. Oh, don't worry. The catalogue says it's perfectly safe for up to a week. It won't cut off circulation or anything. It breathes.

"If you think you can just cut it off, it's going to be more difficult than you think, Dan darling. Inside of the leather is a pretty substantial metal. Besides, you'll like the feel of it under your clothes, I know you will. And I promise to take it off when you come back here, in, say in three days.

"What's the matter, Dan? Is it going to interfere with your social life? Yes, I imagine that would be a hard one to explain away, even in the dark. Don't worry, I'm not going to try to stop you from seeing your little friend. I just want you to have a few days off from both of us to consider what you have there, and what you have here, and the potential difference it would make in your life should you lose one or the other."

"Is this some kind of ultimatum? I don't like threats, Elizabeth."

"No, it's just something I offer up for your consideration. I won't threaten you again with breaking off our relationship. That would be foolish. When I'm ready to, I'll just stop."

He called before he came over three nights later. "I want you to know before I come over," he said, "that I called her and told her it was over. No one can do for me what you do. You're what I need."

I was wary, but a part of me, my vanity most of all, wanted to believe what he said. I accepted his statement as nothing more than a testimonial to my creativity.

No one else could do for him what I could.

When he arrived, he was the same way he'd been on the phone. He started to undress. As I was about to unlock the harness, he said, "You can leave it on for all I care. You can do anything you want. But I'm bound to you no matter what." He moved closer as if to embrace me.

"No," I said, moving back. "No, Dan, that's something you can't have. We aren't going to make love, no matter how sweetly you talk. It's all a con, isn't it? What's the game?"

"No game, Elizabeth. I'm getting tired of playing games. The truth is I stopped seeing the other woman two weeks ago. She was boring me. Sometimes you bore me, too. But there's always the potential of the unexpected with you. I like that. But there are other things I like, too. And you're going to have to give them to me, or I'm going to get them somewhere else."

He kept coming toward me and I kept backing away.

"What's the matter? Don't you like your men in leather?"

Stupidly, I backed up against the wall instead of moving toward the bedroom door. He had me pinned. He savagely ripped off my clothes. For the next hour he raped me again and again.

He threw me onto the bed and spread my legs as far apart as they'd go. He thrust his cock into me with a savagery I would never have expected from him. He was so swollen from anger and lust I almost couldn't take all of him. He raked his hands over my breasts, pinching my nipples roughly, then savaged me with his teeth.

All the while, his cock was in me, ramming me mercilessly. He took me sitting, standing up against the wall, on my back, and on my side. He made me swallow his sperm, then he came all over my face and hair.

He finished the way he'd degraded me once before, by pushing me down onto my stomach and ramming his cock up my anus. The pain was excruciating, but he came quickly and withdrew. I collapsed on the floor, too exhausted to move. I'd put up a fight at first. But I hadn't much of a chance against a man who was a foot taller and nearly a hundred pounds heavier than I, especially a man who imagined he had a score to settle.

He yanked me up by the elbows, like a Samson, blind to everything but his own power.

"Get the key."

I went to the dresser and opened a small Limoges egg, took out the key, and handed it to him. He gave it back to me, slamming it into my right hand.

"Open the locks."

"You do it," I said defiantly.

"You know it won't be the same. Open the locks."

I did what he told me to do.

"That's a good girl," he said as the harness dropped to the floor. Then he dressed. As he was finishing, he said, "You're a good girl, Elizabeth. You give me everything I need. Good girls should be rewarded. Tomorrow night I'll take you out to dinner. Wear something pretty, feminine."

My choices at that point were clear. I could kill him. I could quit the relationship and move to another part of the country. Or I could continue in quest of ultimate victory.

There was never any choice.

So we began a new phase of our relationship—going public. What a sensation we made. The gorgeous couple, each of us so successful in our own right. We were terrifically popular, invited everywhere. And we went. We made the social columns constantly, complete with speculation as to when our nuptials would take place.

Dan's about-to-be-ex must really have felt she was getting her nose rubbed in it. I'm sure that had a lot to do with why Dan was parading me around. Of course, she also had to play the role of victimized wife, so she wasn't shy about telling people there'd been another woman. It helped to have a living, visible body to add truth to her accusations.

Home wrecker, femme fatale, that was me. That sort of thing didn't rate much in the scandal department anymore, so it didn't really hurt Dan or me professionally. If anything, the whole situation enhanced our stature. His wife just looked like the poor, pathetic little homebody, the superficial socialite who couldn't keep up with the needs of her ever-rising star husband, for whom, ironically, someone like me seemed much more of a match. That Dan would turn to a woman who was an independent star in her own right just made him look like more of a man.

I believed the entire sordid mess would give me some sense of triumph. But my battle had never been with Dan's wife. Besides, what had I won?

Nothing much was happening privately now between Dan and me. Everything seemed to center on our public personas. When we were together, we appeared to have a fairly normal relationship, so long as no one looked too closely. When Dan would come to my cottage, it was only long enough to pick me up and drop me off again. It was as if the rest of our relationship had never existed. Our conversations during the brief times we were alone were the polite exchanges of relative strangers.

Then one night he told me about a dinner we were about to have with an old college buddy of his whom I vaguely remembered from Cal. It was one of those rivalry things with Wade. It continued from making touchdowns to making coeds to making it in the business world. Dan was at the top of his company, but Wade had built his own and was on his way to making the Fortune 500.

"He's always been ahead of me. Drives me crazy. He can even out-drink me. The bastard must have the bladder of a camel. I'll hit the john six times and he won't have to budge."

"That must be traumatic," I said sarcastically. "Why don't you wear a diaper? Then you can just sit there and guzzle."

"Very funny."

"I'm serious. Wear one of those adult diapers to dinner and just let it flow, so to speak." If I'd given it some thought, I'd probably have worried about my mind at times like that.

But as the idea sank in, Dan absorbed it more and more and at last said, "You know, that's not such a bad idea."

That look a baby gets on its face when it's done something in its diaper, that's how it was with Dan during our meeting with Wade. Once every hour or so, he'd get this incredibly pleased smile on his face. And I'd know he'd just done it.

Around midnight, Wade, looking as if he had to move quickly, headed straight for the john. You would have thought Dan was back at Cal, getting the winning touchdown of the big game.

The victory made him feel romantic. When he took me home, he made noises about coming in. Like a virgin on the first date, I put him off. I was still biding my time, letting a plan for my next move gestate.

Of one thing I was sure, that letting Dan have his way wasn't a part of my plan for our relationship.

The diaper routine, on the other hand, had intrigued me. I didn't know what he'd done with the rest of the box, but I went out and bought one to have at home. Then I invited Dan to dinner—a huge surprise for him, because even during the early days that was one thing I'd never done.

When he arrived, I told him that what I'd been cooking just hadn't worked out and I hoped he wouldn't mind taking me out to dinner. Then I said I wanted to try a little appetizer before we went. I asked him to take off everything and put on the white, cotton jockey shorts I pulled from the cupboard.

He did as I asked, eagerly, delighted that the games were about to begin anew after my relative inactivity. He looked silly in those shorts, just as most men do, especially if they're a little baggy, as these were.

171

I was at the counter, making up a batch of his favorite cookies. They were the kind his mother had always made for him, and which, of course, I never had. He was enchanted, and, I suspected, trying to make a connection.

"I just wanted to do something special for you," I said, "to celebrate the latest turn of our mutual adventure. My dinner didn't work out, so I thought I'd whip up a batch of your favorite oatmeal cookies, with walnuts and chocolate chips, just the way your mother used to make them."

"Can I have some of the batter?" he asked, grinning like a happy little boy. "That was always the best part."

"Certainly," I said so sweetly, holding out a spoonful for him to take in his mouth. It was like a scene out of a Norman Rockwell.

"Now close your eyes. I have another surprise for you. And don't open them until I say you can."

I pulled out the front, and then the back, of the pants and filled them with the entire contents of the bowl. I snapped the elastic against him and gently pushed him down onto a kitchen chair.

"Now doesn't that feel yummy?" I asked. "I'll bet your mother never made cookies like that."

He didn't say anything, but I could swear he was enjoying the feel of the gooey glob filling his pants and oozing down his legs.

I handed him a diaper the box I had under the sink.

"Here," I said, "put one of these on and let's go."

He seemed about ready to protest and then shrugged. He wrapped the diaper around the mess. I helped him to secure it and to wipe up all the previous leakage. Then he dressed and, looking as elegant and masculine as always, escorted me to L'Etoile for a lovely dinner.

Now I actually thought once was enough of that routine, but I could see Dan wanted more. So there were other nights with a pound or two of butter in his diapers responding to his body heat, and one night of honeying his buns. Then there were the bags of instant mashed potatoes that waited to be rehydrated. That one really disgusted me. I wondered how I'd thought of it.

He loved it. In fact, he seemed to be enjoying all of it more than anything other than physical pain. Dan, it seemed, wasn't just a macho masochist, but a complete sensualist in his way. He was intrigued by the variety of sensations, becoming more and more addicted to them.

At about the point when I realized he was assessing every meal as to its interest potential for wearing rather than eating, I decided that it was time to stop. And since in the obscure rules of our game, if I had chosen the direction, it was my choice to terminate it. He couldn't directly ask for more of the same.

But having reestablished my role as activities director, I was compelled to go on. Dan was implicitly demanding. And I was forced to create new stimuli. In order to pursue ultimate victory, I was forced to constant activity and creativity. Dan, ostensibly the victim in our relationship, did nothing but respond. Basically passive, he constantly reestablished his power. It seemed that there was nothing in my imagination that didn't become satisfying to him, no matter how much it debased him. I continued, hoping that my own victory and ultimate release would emerge.

It had become a necessity for him to have something hidden just below the surface of his perfectly tailored suits—something that, if it were ever revealed, would be devastating. I refused to provide him with any more diaper-filled messes to sit on.

I reverted to a reliance on women's underwear—girdles and garters, reproductions of antique whalebone corsets and bloomers. I was spending more money on his underwear than I ever had on my own.

A variation, sans pain but so cute, were the adult sized Doctor Dentons I found for him with precious little teddy bears cavorting all over them.

Then I switched to the leather harness, a chastity belt adapted to the male form, a gold cock ring, and a copper ensemble of fine webs that connected from head to foot with a series of cuffs. It actually looked like jewelry unless the chains were also in sight.

Fully assembled, it was quite attractive. It seemed rather a shame that I was the only one to see it.

Chapter 11

At last, from the memories of conversations we'd had long ago, in fact from a time before I went to Los Angeles, I plucked the means, I was sure, of defeating him.

He was surprised when I told him to come to my cottage and plan to stay the night. It was the first such invitation in months.

I cleared all the furniture out of the living room. I rented a large projection TV. I covered the floors with simulated Astroturf. At one end of the room I constructed a makeshift goal post. The garden bench was once again pressed into service. By it was a water bucket.

On the bench I'd placed a complete football uniform with the name of Dan's prep school and his number sewn on the jersey.

As soon as he arrived his eyes lit up. I told him to take the uniform into the guest room and change into it. I was wearing plain grey sweats and a pair of cleats. My hair was up under a cap.

When he appeared, I was struck with how splendid Dan looked in that uniform. No wonder women had been throwing themselves at him since puberty, I thought. He was glorious. Looking at him, I nearly lost my purpose. And then I saw him looking at himself in the mirror in the entryway, clearly thinking the same thing.

I moved very carefully. He didn't see or hear me. I quickly activated the video camera I'd set up across the room from the bench. Then I called out loudly.

"Harrington, haul your ass over here."

He jolted out of his self-admiring reverie and did as he was told.

It was beginning. I hoped I could sustain the illusion. I had already tapped into his memory banks. He was concerned about the camera but wasn't about to stop it. The recording was simultaneously being projected big as life onto the huge wall screen.

"You really fucked up today, Harrington," I screamed at him.

"I know, coach. I feel like hell."

"You haven't begun to feel like hell. Just what do you think you were doing out there, you candy-assed sissy?" I wished I could have had the whole football squad assembled for the occasion, as had been the case on the day Dan had told me about.

We entered into the ritual of humiliation. The coach was a sadistic bastard, Dan said. And eventually, when so many students finally complained, he was fired. But that didn't alter what befell the young Dan Harrington that day.

I was determined to make it much more than a berating, accompanying endless push-ups. I stopped him, told him to strip and then start doing them again. When he couldn't do any more, I made him stand up, grabbed his balls, and exclaimed surprise that he had any. I ordered him to masturbate so that everyone could see what he was good for.

It had been going well, but there was a growing, sick ache in my stomach. I found myself shivering with disgust.

"I don't want to do this anymore."

Dan ignored me, or he didn't hear, I didn't know which. He just stood there, jerking off, waiting for my next instructions, the next part of the scenario.

I walked over to the camera and turned it off. He still couldn't grasp that this wasn't part of the game.

"I'm tired, Dan. I don't want to do this anymore. Let's stop. Let's just stop."

"We can't," he protested.

"I can."

"You've said that before. But you need all of this as much as I do. It keeps you going. It's the underpinnings of what keeps you from being just another pretty face on the television screen. The secret we share makes us both complete. It makes us free. It makes us winners. We can't stop. You will not stop."

"Go home, Dan, please. Go home," I said quietly, threateningly, but not in any way that should elicit a power response from him. There was no victory to be achieved.

Except the obvious one. I wanted to stop and he wanted to continue. He had to force me to his will. He took hold of my wrists, grasping them so tightly that I gave a sharp cry of pain. He loosened his hold only slightly.

"I told you, Elizabeth, I don't like threats."

"What are you going to do, Dan? Rape me again to prove that you're a man? Well, do it then, if that's what you need before you go. But do it and go."

There wasn't much excitement in rape by consent. Crestfallen, he pulled on his clothes and left.

For several days I tried to convince myself that I'd won a kind of victory. I wanted to consider my relationship with Dan ended, satisfied that I'd won something. I had denied him. I hadn't set myself up for his demonstration of sexual or psychological prowess. I had simply ended it, on my terms.

But when you'd been living as I had for so many months, it didn't work out that way. I felt as empty as I had that day I'd boarded the plane for L.A. Something essential had been cut out of my life. Nothing its equal was likely to present itself to fill the void.

I had won nothing.

I had given up everything.

I didn't sleep. I had trouble eating. I had strange, abortive fantasies as I lay awake nights. The images continued as I attempted to immerse myself in my work. I felt like a nonentity—a thing without any real purpose. I wasn't a person. I was half a relationship that was no more.

I realized that Dan and I were probably sociopaths, insane in our pursuit of sick desires. But who had we been hurting other than each other? We were consenting adults. It wasn't perversion if both parties involved were doing what they wanted, what they *needed*, to do, was it?

It's not that I had any illusion of love at the base of my need for him. It wasn't hard to stop loving a man once you'd seen him parade around in a bra and girdle.

No, what I craved, what I desperately needed, was what I'd always desired—a decisive victory, a gesture, an action I could use to prove to myself that I was in control of my own destiny.

Dan didn't call me. He couldn't. The next move, if there was to be one, had to be mine. How could it be otherwise? I'd told him that I didn't want to play anymore.

178

If I called him, I had to be ready. It had to be good. New and fresh. In the end, I didn't call. Instead, I sent a note to his apartment. It was an invitation to go with me to Mexico.

Once a year I'd rent a house in a small town in the Yucatan not far from the Mayan ruins at Chichén Itzá. My cottage was actually outside of the town and virtually surrounded by lush jungle. I'd never known the temperature to dip below eighty degrees. The flora was spectacular, the house romantic, isolated. It was always sultry, sensuous, and it usually did wonders for my disposition after a tension-filled year of work.

Usually I went there alone, but I never stayed that way. There were always men, mostly hot-blooded Mexicans. Few Americans came to that part of the country.

I spoke a fair amount of Spanish, certainly enough for what I wanted there. There'd never been a chance of anyone knowing who I was. I was just another horny *gringa* who came south of the border each year to be fucked by strangers who wouldn't carry the fetters of emotional involvement. It had always worked well. There was an occasional repeat from year to year, but it was implicit that we were to remain just as much strangers to each other as when we'd met. It was simply a matter of two people getting what they wanted and moving on.

How I wished I could have lived my whole life that way.

A jungle setting had yielded interesting results with Dan before. That was why I decided to try the real thing. This time, though,. the only wild cat in the forest would be me. I had a plan. I couldn't be sure of the results, but I put things in motion toward my desired end. I felt more in control than I'd ever been.

I felt Dan and I were moving toward some predestined end when I put the invitation in his mailbox.

I offered him three possible weeks in the next two months when we could take the vacation. He accepted and chose the earliest one. My joy was boundless. I told him I'd take care of the tickets and make all the other arrangements. He needed only to get his tourist permit and comfortable clothes suitable for the warm weather.

I was sure he thought I was taking him to Puerto Vallarta or Cancún, where we could have our strange little rituals in private and then socialize with the rest of the beautiful people.

I had to admit he looked magnificent in his white silk shirt and slacks the day he met me at the airport. We flew to Mexico City, then took a shuttle flight to Mérida.

In my mind was an image of an ancient pool, not far from where we were going, where virgins had been sacrificed to the gods. The idea appealed to me; this was, after all, going to be a virgin experience for Dan Harrington. It would be a sacrifice to the demons that now ruled our lives.

After dinner in Mérida, we boarded the train for our village. We would reach it late the next afternoon.

I hadn't planned anything for our day on the rails, but I felt there should be something to make the night interesting and to build anticipation for what was to come. So just as the train pulled out and we'd gotten settled in our private compartment, I crept up behind Dan and slipped a gold slave collar around his neck. I locked it shut, enjoying his look of surprise.

It could have passed for jewelry, and it was narrow enough and loose enough to be comfortable. Of course it wasn't *normal* jewelry—it locked with a tiny gold key and also had a jeweled hoop to which a chain could be attached. I attached a long one, rather like a dog's leash, after Dan had undressed. I chained him to the lower berth, kindly allowing him enough slack so that he could get about to any corner of the compartment and the john at one end of it.

That was all there was to that night. I knew that Dan was disappointed, but I didn't want to waste time or energy. I wanted to be completely rested for the next day and the rest of the week.

In the morning, after we'd both cleaned up and I'd dressed, I had him push up the top berth so we had plenty of room to sit on the lower one. I left the "Do Not Disturb" sign hanging outside the door. I'd brought along sandwiches and bottled water, so we had everything we needed in the way of provisions. I could proceed unhindered in my work.

I opened the curtains so that we could enjoy the view. Dan was a trifle unnerved by that. But I assured him that we'd made the last stop before our own and that even if anyone did see him as we passed by, it would hardly be anyone we knew. That, along with a certain barely concealed pleasure at the possibility of discovery, increased greatly the appeal of the situation.

"You need a shave," I told him, running my hand across his chin. "I'm going to give it to you, but a little differently."

I'd brought a portable electric pot with with me, and plugged its converter into the socket next to us. The wax I'd already put in it began to heat and melt.

"You'll love this," I crooned. "You won't have to shave again all week." I applied the wax to his face, under his arms, to his legs. Then having completed that, I removed the golden forest from around his genitals. He winced during the operation, opened his mouth to speak, but said nothing.

"There, now," I said, enjoying the results of my labor. "You're as smooth as a newborn baby, or a beautiful young lady." He was obviously excited; his cock rose mightily from the now-smooth plain of his lower abdomen.

I went on to paint his finger- and toenails, telling him to sit perfectly still so I didn't smear the polish. I did his face next, applying the makeup with a heavier hand than we had at home. I was pleased to see that he was wearing his hair a little longer than he had in the past. With a little teasing and spraying, plus a fabulous pair of dangling earrings, he looked quite splendid. He didn't need a wig at all.

Finally, I pulled out a suitcase full of women's clothes in his size, choosing a one-piece bathing suit that was cut so high at the legs that it barely covered his stunning ass. I inserted a codpiece that acted as a minimizer for his penis and balls. When he had it on, even with his broad shoulders and large hands and feet, he looked like a magnificent, if Amazonian, woman.

I unfastened the chain and let him go to the mirror to admire the effect.

Before, he'd always been a kind of caricature. This was very nearly real. If I had taken a picture of him and presented it to him later, I'm not sure he would have recognized himself. A bit of padding for the top of the suit, a pair of sandals, a wraparound skirt and brightly colored silk blouse, and he was delicious to behold.

Then I undressed. I put on a string bikini, which Dan didn't seem to appreciate. "I have to match the competition I'm going to be with," I said sweetly. "I want someone to notice me when we go to the hotel pool."

"I thought we were staying in a private house."
His eyes almost bugged from his head.

"We are, but I thought we'd eat a late lunch at the
hotel in the village first, then a nice dip in their pool
before we go home. The pool at the house isn't nearly as large. Besides, I want to show you off."

I couldn't imagine what the train crew who'd seen
us boarding thought when they saw us detrain. They
probably wrote us off as two crazy foreigners, which,
I suppose, we were.

I put the suitcases in a locker at the station and
summoned a cab to take us to the hotel. We had a
lovely lunch on the veranda. Afterward, Daniella
worked on her tan while I swam.

The men were all over us, drawn as much, maybe
more, to the big, healthy, blonde beauty as they were
to me.

I could see that, despite his misgivings, Dan was
enjoying the attention. It was amazing what his ego
could respond to.

He didn't try to do a female impersonation with
his voice, but softened it more or less within his own
register. He was completely captivating.

As the sun began to set, I told him that it was best
that we head for my hacienda. There would be plenty
of time during the week to explore the rest of the
charming little village and the local environs.

Dan may have been dressed like a woman,
responding flirtatiously to the attentions of various
men, but I could see that his eyes still wandered to
several of the pretty señoritas around the pool. I
guessed he was contemplating how he could get the
makeup and polish off, get into his own clothes, and
explore the opportunities.

But I had very different opportunities in mind for
him. I allowed him to continue in his fantasies undis-

183

turbed, while I thought about the soon-to-be realities.

We returned to the train station and I retrieved our luggage.

In about fifteen minutes we arrived at the house. I sent Dan in to tell the maid that we'd arrived, while I took care of the driver. Maria came at once to help with the luggage.

"*La otra señora*," was exploring the house, she said.

"*Esta bien*," I assured her. I instructed her to take all of the luggage to the large bedroom.

When Dan and I were alone, he remarked, "You didn't tell me about that sweet young thing. She's a real pastry. How old is she?"

"Maria?" I replied absently. "Oh, I suppose she's twenty-two or twenty-three."

"Don't worry," he tried to assure me. "I'm just enjoying the sights. I'll be a good boy, even after I get out of all this. I wouldn't dream of concentrating on anything or anybody else but you while we're on this adventure."

His arrogance never ceased to fascinate me.

"Oh, it's fine with me if you want to try," I replied. "But a good boy isn't exactly what you're going to be on this trip."

"Listen, Elizabeth, this getup was a good joke for arrival. I don't know what else you have planned, but this aspect of it has gone far enough. You dictate the rules of the game in private, for now. But I'm not going to waste a whole week down here running around like this."

Dan was back. He thought he could assume command.

He was wrong.

"Dan, count the suitcases. Three of them, right?

Two are mine and one is yours. But check it out; it's not the one you brought." I opened it for him. It was the one filled with the tropical wardrobe I had selected for him.

"Cut the crap, Elizabeth. Where's my luggage?"

"In a locker at the train station. I've already put the key away for safekeeping until we're ready to go back. So don't get any ideas. You just take this bag into the other room and unpack while I finish in here."

For a moment I believed he was going to kill me. The color rose in his face until I thought his head would burst. I egged him on.

"And wait until you see some of the pretty underwear I chose for you. None of that iron-maiden stuff. I want you to be perfectly comfortable and relaxed. Everything is silk, your favorite. There's even the cutest little teddy and dance pants ensemble in midnight blue. You'll love it. Now shoo; I want to finish and take a nice, soothing bubble bath. You might want to do the same."

I breathed a sigh of relief as he did as he was told. He was mine.

We dined late that night at home, Dan wearing the most "masculine" pieces of the wardrobe I'd packed for him—a cotton pants outfit in pale green. But it didn't matter. He looked like a luscious dish of lime sherbet that any man would be proud to be seen with. I told him so.

He grimaced at me and, throughout dinner, continued to eye Maria hungrily. How galling it must have been when Maria asked me if it was all right for her boyfriend to visit after she'd finished cleaning up. I told her it was and that she should feel free to entertain him on the veranda if she liked.

I translated for Dan, who didn't speak Spanish.

185

His expression delighted me. My mockery only served to infuriate him. I no longer had any doubts that my plan was going to proceed, and succeed, as expected. After a few not-terribly-pleasant words from Dan, we went to our respective bedrooms.

I knew it would take a day or two, but he'd cheer up and get more into the mood of things. Dan, as I well knew, was very adaptable.

As I lay in my bed, enjoying the gentle sounds of the night, I could hear Maria singing to a tune her boyfriend played on the guitar. It was enchanting. Then the music stopped and there was laughter, a bit of conversation, followed only by the squeaking of the large porch swing.

Dan's bedroom was far closer to the veranda than mine. He'd hear more of the luscious details. I fell asleep smiling.

I left him alone most of the next morning, letting him sleep nearly until lunchtime. Then, tapping gently on his door, I called out, "Daniella, you're going to miss the whole day. Now get up and make yourself pretty."

Grim, but nonetheless attractive, it was indeed Daniella who emerged from the bedroom a half hour later.

"Now, don't pout," I said patronizingly. "Cheer up. I have special plans for us tonight."

But that didn't help. Dan sulked most of the day. He lounged by our pool, but covered himself almost from head to toe with a large beach towel. I let him be and did a bit of sunbathing and relaxing.

That night, I arranged the ensembles for both of us. Mine was a relatively sedate, sarong type of dress of very subdued pastels. I wore simple jewelry.

For Daniella, it was quite a different matter. I had laid out a hot pink backless halter and a rose-colored skirt that clung to his shapely ass. He wore simple gold clip-on earrings, the slave collar, and a bracelet. He was too divine.

We went to my favorite cantina in town. It had the kind of atmosphere that encouraged everyone to drink a little too much. The spirit of the place was intoxicating. It had a rock band that played familiar songs with a Latin twist. One of their tricks was to emphasize the already-intense rhythms by banging on something that resembled a cowbell. I'd been there on nights when it seemed as if that bell timed the heartbeats of everyone in the room. It had amazed me that the combination of the music, the drinking, the heat, that bell, and the mounting level of shared passion hadn't turned the whole thing into an orgy.

But the patina of civilization that hung over public places always prevailed and restrained the revellers. Such a pity.

The atmosphere was already pretty heady when Dan and I arrived. I could see every man in the place turn to look at us. It was almost a given in Mexico that there were always more men than women in social environments, especially in a backwater town like the one we were in. Macho tradition prevailed—the men left their good women at home while they went in search of bad ones. Americans were always strong candidates for that classification.

We were approached immediately, but I didn't see anyone that was right for us. And to be kind, I wanted to give Dan time to acclimate himself to the situation before I "encouraged" him to dance with one of the macho Mexican men bidding for his attention.

I ordered margaritas and suggested that he drink up so that he could relax and enjoy himself. The alcohol was just beginning to take effect when we were approached by a pair of well-dressed, well-behaved, very attractive men.

I immediately accepted the invitation to dance from the shorter of the two; Alfonso was his name. The other, who called himself Cesar, was at least five inches shorter than Daniella, but seemed determined, nevertheless, to conquer the statuesque blonde.

At first Dan demurred. I think it disturbed him that the two men looked like the kind of people he could easily meet in the course of business. The association seemed to be just a bit too strong for him; it threatened his illusion of his strength, his power.

I wasn't surprised though, that after another drink and persuasions all around, Dan at last consented to head for the dance floor with Cesar.

When the band switched to one of its few slow songs of the evening, Alfonso was polite, holding me no closer than propriety, or what passed for propriety in this environment, permitted. Only when I smiled at him and made no motion to pull away from him did he settle into a more intimate posture.

Cesar had far less reluctance. He held Dan so close that I was afraid that, even with all the protective covering, he might get a poke from Dan's privates. But all seemed to be well. I could see him whispering into Dan's ear, his hand slipping steadily down the curve of Dan's back.

It was all I could do to pay attention to my own partner. As he nuzzled my neck and broached the subject of sleeping with me, I gave him my full attention and tentative consent. When the rock music resumed, I suggested that we remove ourselves to the balcony and discuss it where it was more quiet. He was happy to comply.

"You are so attractive," I said, letting my hand

find its way, as if by accident, to his crotch. His cock was erect, straining at the fabric. "And believe me, there's nothing I would like better than to get into bed with you this instant. But there's a little problem."

He pulled back from me with a jolt. "Oh, no," I said, "not with me. I assure you. I'm perfectly healthy, as I'm sure you are." He nodded affirmatively. "And I know you wouldn't mind using a condom. I have plenty of them in the house for situations such as this one." He didn't mind that. But, he asked anxiously, "*Que es la problema*?" In his anxiety, he lapsed from his otherwise fluent use of English.

I shrugged. "*Mi amiga Daniella es mi amigo*, Dan. Actually, he's my cousin. He's had this problem for years. He's very straight at home, very definitely in the closet. Because of his professional stature he can't afford even the slightest hint of his unorthodox sexual preferences. Our family would never accept him as a homosexual transvestite. It's all very sad, really.

"So from time to time, he comes to my place to relax and dress up. The risk of scandal keeps him celibate, except in out-of-the-way locations. When we travel together, usually I just let him go to his own kind of places. But there's nothing like that here. We just hoped that we might be lucky and find the right kind of person for him. I promised him if nothing happened in a couple of days, we'd go to Mexico City where we do know of one or two very nice places that cater to gentlemen of his preference."

I ran my fingers through Alfonso's hair.

"So you see, I do have a problem and so will your friend, if he proceeds."

Alfonso nodded. "Cesar wouldn't like to be surprised. But he is not without a sense of adventure. He might want to try it."

"I don't want to get Dan's hopes up, so let's not say anything yet. Perhaps you could talk to Cesar privately. If he does agree, and that would be wonderful, we can all go back to my hacienda. This could be such a happy night for Dan…iella."

"My dear lady, to be close to you I would persuade my friend to make love to your dog if need be. As for your beautiful cousin, *no hay problema.*"

When we returned inside, Dan and I excused ourselves, ostensibly to powder our noses. I deliberately took a great deal of time praising Dan for his ability to carry off the charade. Not surprisingly, now that he felt comfortably in control of it all, he was enjoying this new experience.

When we returned to the table, Alfonso suggested that we all go back to my hacienda for a little quiet conversation. He would invite us to their hotel, he said, but then we would be in a small room. Plus he didn't think that nice ladies such as we would want to go to a man's hotel room under any circumstances. I made some pretense of considering the offer, then said yes.

Dan looked dismayed. He stammered that he was extremely tired. But he was outnumbered and outmaneuvered. Alfonso drove us in his car; Dan and Cesar were in the back. Alfonso had no doubt that my beaming smile was all for him as I caught sight in the mirror of Cesar running his hand gently up Dan's thigh.

When we got to the house, I put soft music on the stereo and poured wine for everyone. Dan and Cesar danced. Alfonso and I necked on the sofa. We were all in the advanced stages of inebriation. Alfonso wanted to go to the bedroom, but that wasn't what I had in mind.

I pulled off my dress. Underneath I was wearing

only the flimsiest of panties, guaranteed by the manufacturer to rip at the slightest touch. I'd worn no bra or stockings.

I put Alfonso's hand just inside the waistband and pulled away from him. The panties functioned exactly as promised, ripping in his hand. He was in such a state of ecstasy that I don't think he could have stopped if we'd been in the middle of Candlestick Park. In an instant he was out of his own clothes.

His cock grew stiff as he covered every inch of my body with his eyes. First he shoved what looked to be a foot-long salami into my mouth. He came quickly, coating my mouth with his jism, but I kept at it until he hardened once again.

He drove his dick into my dripping tunnel, working me with long, smooth strokes. He liked to see my tits swaying with each thrust, and he varied the tempo to see the differences in their movements. Then he put his hands on them for support and banged me for all I was worth. He came in torrents.

I could see out of the corner of my eye that Dan and Cesar had stopped dancing and were mesmerized watching us. Dan had seen tapes of me with other men. He'd heard the sounds of my lovemaking first hand, but this was the first time he'd had an unobstructed view of the full live show.

I have no doubt Alfonso believed that I considered him to be the world's greatest lover. He'd been very good. My expressions of passion and appreciation for his prowess were unending.

But it was Cesar and Daniella I wanted to see. Their show was just beginning.

Cesar was caressing and kissing Dan. And yes, Dan was responding. But then Cesar began to undress him and Dan looked as if he would panic.

"It's all right, my darling," Cesar said, "I know

everything. And I don't mind. I have done this kind of thing before. You will find me a gentle lover, even of this nature." He proceeded to remove Dan's outer clothes.

In his high-cut bikinis Dan really had fabulous legs, especially since I'd shaven them. He would have looked appealing to just about anyone of any preference. Cesar was delighted. In a short time they were worked up into a complete frenzy, oblivious to our presence. Cesar pulled down Dan's bikinis but left on the codpiece. He took off his own clothes, and then gently moved Dan to the floor, caressing him gently, positioning him on all fours.

Dan's eyes were on me as Cesar proceeded to thrust his penis into a part of Dan's anatomy that I doubt had ever previously been used for that particular purpose. Dan gasped, then let out a sharp cry of pain, or passion, or both. Cesar rocked with a steady motion, plunging into and out of Dan's ass. His rhythm increased; he pushed harder and harder until his testicles slapped against the buttocks he'd violated. Shortly thereafter the color rose in his chest and face and I knew he'd come. Tears were streaming down Dan's face.

It was all over very quickly. Then Dan was on his back, Cesar still at his side caressing and kissing him. Dan didn't do much, but he seemed happy enough. When Cesar straddled Dan's chest and offered his limp cock to Dan's mouth, I whispered to Alfonso that I thought we should go to bed. In my bedroom we made love once more and then went to sleep.

In the morning, I was the first one up. I quietly opened Dan's door. He and Cesar were wrapped around each other in the bed.

Alfonso and Cesar stayed most of the day, but we were all a little played out. Still, the experience had been electrifying and we parted amicably—they, to return to Mexico City, us to the enjoyment of our passions in the tropical setting.

When they'd gone, Dan and I didn't talk about the encounter. We retired to our own beds.

At breakfast the following morning, I handed Dan the key to the locker in the train station. "You're free to do what you want with it," I told him. "Go and get your clothes and continue the stay as yourself. Or go and get your clothes and go home. It's completely up to you."

He didn't say anything.

For the next four days the key sat on his dresser as Daniella continued to appear. I left Dan pretty much on his own from then on.

I didn't find anyone else I wanted to sleep with, but Dan didn't have any trouble in that department. I couldn't be sure who his partners were. I saw only the final one the morning before we left, when I happened to get up especially early.

It was a young Mexican man stealthily leaving the hacienda. He looked frightened when he saw me, but I assured him in Spanish that it was okay and that I hoped he'd had a good time with my cousin.

He smiled nervously and said that he had. "Did he give you any money?" I asked.

"No," he said.

"That isn't nice," I said, "wait just a minute." I went to my purse and brought him one hundred dollars worth of pesos. Beaming with appreciation, he thanked me and then was quickly out the door.

Dan was so cheap.

The next day we started the trek back home. We picked up Dan's suitcase at the train station. It amused me that Daniella didn't turn back into Dan until the last hour before the train arrived at Mérida.

We didn't talk much. Outside of the context of a particular game, we rarely did anymore. I would have loved to have known what was going on in his mind, what was next for Dan Harrington.

I didn't have any immediate plans for him. I'd decided that he might need a rest to think things through. How would he face the world as Dan Harrington, master of his fate? He was a man who had taken it in the ass and loved it.

I could sense my imminent victory.

Dan was quiet through both flights, thinking, meditating. I wondered if he was considering how he could get more of this new thing he craved. In San Francisco, with appearances to keep and caution an essential, he would be like a drowning man. There'd be water, water all around, and not a drop that poor Dan dared to drink.

I almost felt sorry for him, for what I'd done to him.

When we arrived in San Francisco and cleared customs, his car, driver, and secretary were waiting for us.

"Dave," he said, handing the driver the baggage tags, "you go around and wait for the luggage. Miss Winslow, let's get started with the phone messages first. Oh, Elizabeth, why don't you get a magazine or something to read on the ride back? I'm going to be too busy to pay any further attention to you."

He turned his back on me, dismissed me.

He'd resumed wearing his mantle of power.

Chapter 12

A week passed. Neither of us contacted the other. Then Dan called me and asked me to dinner.

Once again, we embarked on normal public dating. Once or twice Dan made half-spirited sexual overtures, responding indifferently to my rejection of them. I was an ornament again that served a purpose for him. I reminded myself that he performed the same function for me, that moreover, I still had a quest ahead of me.

The only vestige of our private relationship was the thin gold slave collar. I never offered him the key, nor did he request it. He seemed to like wearing it as some sort of defiant symbol.

A few days later he told me that he had to go to Vancouver for a five-day conference. He asked me if I wanted to come with him.

"Just as an ordinary couple," he said, smiling. "I'd like to have your company."

"You mean you'd like to have me there as an attractive appendage."

"Whatever you say, but Vancouver is a beautiful city and I thought you might like to get away for a few days."

"I'll think it over," I responded cautiously. I thought about it. And I said yes.

I had, as they say, never looked more beautiful than I did during the days of that trip. There weren't a lot of wives or lovers along, so I stood out even more in the group than I would have normally.

At the welcoming party, especially when we were dancing, I hung on to Dan in such a way as to leave little doubt in anyone's mind that he was getting a lot of action from me.

Especially gratifying for Dan, under these circumstances, was the presence of his old drinking buddy, Wade, who was recently divorced and unaccompanied. I really turned it on over Dan whenever he was around. Dan loved it.

As always, he began to buy the illusion. The time was right, he was convinced, the second night. We'd entered our hotel suite and I let it go on a bit, allowing him to kiss me, touch me. I responded sufficiently to be sure he was really aroused.

Then I pulled away, looked at him directly and said frigidly, "Playtime is over Dan. This time the game is only for the public." I turned my back on him and flounced into my own bedroom.

A minute later I could hear the shower running in his bathroom—with very cold water, I imagined.

The next day, when he came back from his meetings, he found the door of my bedroom ajar. There were strange sounds coming from inside. He pushed open the door to discover one of the bellboys burying his cock in my throbbing cunt. Dan went away without commenting on the situation.

The following evening I left my door wide open. In case he was able to resist temptation and go to his own room or leave, I wanted to be sure he wouldn't miss the action. I lay on the bed with two women

196

(prostitutes, but I didn't tell him that). We were all nude, although one of them wore garters and stockings.

When Dan arrived, I invited him in to watch us play. But I didn't extend an invitation to join in the fun. He stayed only a short time.

The next revelation was of me with a male prostitute, this time so identified and introduced. When Dan walked in, careful not to go near my bedroom, he opened the door of his room to find me on all fours. I was chained by my ankles and wrists to the bed in paroxysms of ecstasy while a baby-faced twenty-three-year-old boy paddled me. The sounds of the whacks against my throbbing ass filled the air.

Actually, I hated it. The S&M scene wasn't for me. But it was worth the pain for what it was doing to Dan. He couldn't make himself leave or stop watching. The boy unchained me and then we fucked in more positions than I had ever imagined possible. His energy was boundless and his cock inexhaustible. I took him in my mouth, my pussy, and even in my ass.

I did enjoy that and almost forgot that Dan was there. When we were finished, the boy and I, laughing, went arm and arm into Dan's bathroom to shower. When we came back out, Dan was gone.

I paid off my stud, dressed, and went downstairs to find Dan. He was in the hotel bar. We went to dinner with several of his colleagues. I was exquisite and charming. In public, I behaved adoringly toward my man.

There was only one day to go. I had saved the best for last. I suppose Dan could have loused it up by not coming upstairs directly after his meetings, but he never would have done that. He had to play the game all the way through.

Dan entered the living room of the suite to find me naked on the sofa. Wade was on top of me ramming his cock down my throat with reckless abandon. I'd given him a gold chain to wear around his neck; a pair of Dan's blue silk briefs lay on the floor. His dear pal had made it into the Fortune 500 and now he was making it into me.

Dan didn't say anything, just turned as if to leave.

"Oh, don't go, Dan," I said. "We were just finishing."

Wade got off me calmly, drawing his slacks on without putting on Dan's briefs.

"Sorry, buddy," he said amiably, "but you know I never could resist a good thing. And this was a very, very good thing. I'll see you at the stag party later, if you're still coming."

He turned to me and kissed my hand. "I certainly hope I'll see you again, any time, any place."

The he left.

Dan said, "I thought we'd agreed that this was to be an ordinary trip as an ordinary couple."

"That's right," I said brightly, "and you've been cuckolded just like an ordinary man."

"Bitch," he said.

"Yes, I know, and that's what keeps you interested. So let's not argue. Besides, I want to help you to get ready for tonight."

"What do you mean?"

"Well, darling, this week has to have been a strain on your libido. And I know firsthand what your business parties are like. So I just want to make sure that you don't do anything that I wouldn't want you to do.

"I have something special for you that'll ensure that you'll think of me the whole time. If you do, and if you're a good boy, there may be special rewards for you when you come home tonight.

198

"When you open the door, you'll find a lady or a tiger. And you'll love either one. It might be a whole new game. Think of the possibilities. Wouldn't you like to do the kind of thing that man did to me? Think of it—me tied up, Dan, completely under your power."

As I explained all of this to him I was still completely nude, and frequently rubbed up against him, the musky smell of another man still on my body.

"But even if things are going to change, we have the old game to finish. I have something I want you to wear. I'm even going to help you to dress." I opened his fly and pulled down his slacks and requisite blue briefs. His enraged cock sprang free.

"Come on, darling, just step out of them. And let me help you put on the others." I fastened a very pretty black and red garter belt around his waist and attached red lace stockings to it. Then I helped him put on a flimsy little pair of red bikinis.

"Now, then," I said admiringly, "you look absolutely fetching. Which suit and shirt are you wearing? I'll get them for you."

He looked perfect in his steel grey suit and blue shirt. They brought out the blue of his eyes.

Dan went to meet his fate.

With the help of Dan's good buddy, Wade, I was once again the surprise attraction of the big event. There were female dancers, but they only danced and teased. Then they became handmaidens to the star, a masked lady who appeared in full eighteenth century court garb, all very regal. To the music of that century, but set to a pounding rock beat, I began to strip. There was so much to take off, it must have seemed like hours passed to the shouting crowd of executive barbarians.

When I was down to my own modern-day pearl

pink bra, panties, garter belt, stockings, and spiked heels, I dismissed the other women. I descended from the stage to where the men were and gave them various opportunities to touch me in various places.

Like animals they rose to their feet, grabbing for me. I let one of them lift me onto a table and caress my pussy as I unhooked and removed my bra, flinging it to another table where the occupants nearly killed each other to catch it. My breasts swung freely; my hard nipples jutted prominently.

I allowed another group of them, led by Wade, to lift me into the air. As they held me, I pulled off the stockings one by one, wrapping them around the necks of those closest to me. They set me down on a table, and I pulled the garter belt out from inside the panties and tossed it in the air.

I found Dan and focused entirely on him. I began to move to the rhythm of the music, putting my hands inside the panties as if to remove them. Instead, I simply fondled my twat. Wade lifted me down from the table, and I went directly to my primary target. I rubbed up against Dan and then massaged his crotch.

Silence descended over the room. They anticipated a fucking. The violent pulse of the music reverberated from the walls, as I danced in front of and against Dan. I took his hand and guided it into my panties. The smell of sex permeated the atmosphere.

Dan's peers were like a pack of rutting animals who must accord the strongest stag the right to the first mating.

A man possessed, Dan began his own attack, the rest of the men cheering him on. I began to move toward the stage, trying to lead him. But then Dan, ever conscious of the need for a powerful gesture, swept me up in his arms and carried me there, setting me down on the antique chaise of the boudoir setting.

In a completely mindless state now, he began to open his pants. I stopped him. The cheers and catcalls were reaching a fevered pitch.

"No," I said, so that only he could hear. Standing up, I told him, "If you want me, get on your knees and beg for me, or I'll walk away now. All you have to do to show all of your colleagues what a great stud you are is to get on your knees for just a few seconds. And then you can do anything you want with me, here or anywhere.

"Think of it, Dan. I'll be your slave from now on. All you have to do is get on your knees this one time. If you don't, I'll walk away. Now. And you'll look like an impotent fool. Make a decision, Dan. Get on your knees, Dan. Now."

I held my breath, as slowly, oh, so slowly, Dan sank to his knees. There was silence again from everyone in the room.

"That's good," I said, "that's very good." I opened his fly and began pulling down his slacks. I knew that he was completely in my power, completely detached from whatever it was that made him Dan Harrington. He was almost in a trance, doing exactly as he was told.

A ripple of laughter started and grew as the sight of Dan's fully grown cock emerged from his crotchless panties. The red straps of the garters came into view. Best of all, spelled out in glittering rhinestones across his beautiful ass, on a covering of flimsy, cheap red nylon, were the words, HOT PANTS.

The laugher turned into a roar of derision. Dan was frozen. As he knelt there, I turned to the audience, pulled off my panties and—waving them in a victorious salute—sent them sailing in Wade's direction. I stood there for just a second to receive the applause and cheers. Then I stepped back onto a small, transparent platform that gracefully ascended into the air.

I don't even know if Dan comprehended what I was saying as I faded from his sight.

"Good-bye, Dan" I called. "The game is over. I told you I would never threaten. I would just stop. Now I can."

I watched him in his abasement as I rose into the air. I finally knew the taste of complete, irrevocable victory.

I would never lose again.

ROVINCETOWN UMMER

$7.95

dsay welsh

ISBN 0-9716384-2-X

the casual encounters of women on the prowl to the enduring erotic bonds between overs, these women will set your senses on fire!

lesbian libido explodes in this book of short stories written by and about the rs of Sappho. This completely original collection is devoted exclusively to white-desire between women. In the title story, a writer shares a passionate but ossible love with an artist in a sleepy seaside town. From the casual encounters omen on the prowl to the enduring erotic bond between old lovers, the women of incetown Summer will set your senses on fire!

AN With a MAID

$7.95

onymous

ISBN 0-937609-25-0

at erotic fiction begins and ends with this novel."

—Evergreen Review

ultimate epic of sexual domination. In the "snuggery", a padded soundproofed room ped with wall pulleys, a strap down table, and a chair with hand and leg shackles. The ng pervert, Jack, bends beautiful Alice to his will. She corrupts her maid and her best d into lesbianism, then the three girls lure a voluptuous mother and her demure hter into the snuggery for a forcible seduction and orgy.
aps, the all-time hottestbook!

HE BLUE ROSE

$7.95

on tyler

ISBN 0-9716384-8-9

n Tyler's words evoke a world of heady sensuality, where fantasies are fearlessly red and dreams gloriously realized.

-Penthouse

ale of a modern sorority - fashioned after a Victorian girl's school. Ignited to the ts of passion by erotic tales of the Victorian Age, a group of lusty young women are uraged to act out their forbidden fantasies - all under the turelage of Mistresses Emily ustine, two avid practitioners of hard-core discipline!

MASTERING MARY SUE $7

mary love
ISBN 0-9716384-C

Mary Sue is a rich nymphomaniac whose husband is determined to pervert her, decl.
her mentally incompetent, and gain control of her fortune. He brings her to a castle
Europe, where, to Mary Sue's delight, they have stumbled on an unimaginably deprav
sex cult!

ALEXANDER **TROCCHI** $7

thongs
ISBN 0-937609-26

Spain, perhaps more than any other country in the world, is the land of passion ar
death. And in Spain life is cheap, from that glittering tragedy in the bullring to the c
thrust of the stiletto in a narrow street in a Barcelona slum. No, this death would not
called for further comment had it not been for one striking act. The naked woman had
her end in a way he had never seen before — a way that had enormous sexual significa
My God she had been...

TABITHA'S TEASE $7

robin wilde
ISBN 0-9716384-9

"If you have ever fantasized about being dominated by a sorority of beautiful co
women, then used as their sex toy, then this is the book for you."
—Mistress Solange

When you're a helpless male captive of the notorious sorority girls of Tau Zeta Rho, y
in for a deliciously devilish week of the most exotic and erotic torments these imagina
wicked co-eds can devise. And if you get the infamous Tabitha as your tormentrix, y
find yourself hovering on the excruciating edge with each new perverse twist o
insatiable imagination.
Think it's a man's world? Guess again. With Tabitha around, no man gets what he v
until she's completely satisfied—and maybe, not even then.

CINDERELLA

$7.95

ian beresford

ISBN 0-9716384-1-1

wildly decadent and completely original erotic fairy tale"
—Dr. Pascale Solange

Magical exploration of the erotic potential of this famous fairy tale. Titian Beresford mphs with castle dungeons and tightly corseted ladies-in-waiting, naughty Viscounts impossibly cruel masturbatrixes-nearly every conceivable method of kinky arousal is lored and described in vivid detail. A fetishist's dream and a masochist's delight.

UDITH BOSTON

$7.95

ian beresford

ISBN 0-9716384-6-2

ew, unexpurgated edition! Naughty Edward's compulsive carnal experiments never go unished by the severe Judith Boston. Edward would be lucky to get the stodgy npanion he thinks his parents have hired for him. Instead, an exquisite woman arrives is door, and from the top of her tightly bound bun to the tips of her impossibly high s, Judith Boston is in complete control..

HE LIMOUSINE

$7.95

t. morley

ISBN 0-9716384-4-6

cious Brenda was enthralled with her roommate Kristi's illicit sex life: a never-ending de of men who satisfied Kristi's desire to be dominated. While barely admitting she ed these desires, Brenda issued herself the ultimate challenge — a trip into total mission, beginning in the long, white limousine where Kristi first met the Master. owing in the footsteps of her lascivious roommate, Brenda embarks on the erotic ney of her life.

ORDERING IS EASY

orders can be placed by calling our toll-free number
PHONE: 800.729.6423/FAX: 310.532.7001/E.MAIL: magiccarpetbooks@aol.com
or mail this coupon to:
Magic Carpet Books
15608 South New Century Drive
Gardena, CA 90248

QTY.	TITLE	NO.	PRICE

We never sell, give or trade any of our customer's names

	SUBTOTAL	
	POSTAGE + HANDLING	
	TOTAL	

In the U.S., please add $1.50 for the first book and 75¢ for each additional book;
in Canada, add $2.00 for the first book and $1.25 for each additional book.
Foreign countries: add $4.00 for the first book and $2.00 for each additional book.
Sorry, no C.O.D. orders.
Please make all checks payable to Magic Carpet Books
Payable in U.S. Currency only. CA state residents add 8.25% sales tax.
Please allow 4-6 weeks for delivery.

Name: _____

Address: _____

City: _____ State _____ Zip _____

Telephone: [   ] _____

E.mail: _____

Payment: ☐ check ☐ money order ☐ visa ☐ mc ☐ amex ☐ discover ☐ diners club

Card No: _____